THE MENDOCINO BEACH HOUSE

NELLIE BROOKS

Merpaper Press LLC

ISBN-13: 978-1-958957-14-1

Published by Merpaper Press LLC

Edited by Karen Meeus Editing

CONTENTS

CHAPTER 1

B eth opened the door and stepped into the morning light of Mendocino Beach. The salty air carried the scent of flowers—roses her late husband, Ben, had lovingly planted before he died. They thrived in the warm summers and tolerated the mild coastal winters of Northern California. Now, the roses towered over her, their vines climbing over the trellis that shielded the patio from the sea breeze, their velvety, voluptuous blooms cascading down the sides.

She reached out to support one of the heavy blooms, but a thorn pricked her finger. Beth pulled her hand back, watching as a small drop of blood formed. Instinctively, she lifted her hand as if to show Ben, a habit born from years of shared moments. But reality quickly returned—he was gone. Ben had died years ago.

Beth had made progress. Her grief wasn't the constant, suffocating presence it once was; now it ebbed and flowed like the tides washing against the cliffs beyond the garden. She was learning to accept his absence, but it was hardest here at home, where every corner, every scent, every bloom was a reminder of him. His memory was woven into the very fabric of this place—the house he'd built, the flowers he'd planted, the life they'd shared.

She pulled a tissue from the pocket of her white bathrobe and wrapped it around her finger. She'd need good gardening gloves to trim the thorny stalks; their beauty was undeniable, but so was the danger of their thick thorns.

The entire garden needed attention. Like the house, it had been Ben's passion project, while Beth had simply enjoyed the fruits of his labor. Now, without his careful hands, the bushes, boxwoods, floral beds, and lawns slipped into disrepair. Even the house itself showed signs of neglect. There were fine cracks in a bathroom wall, peeling paint, brittle wood Beth hadn't noticed until recently.

She sat on the stairs by the sliding doors, hugging her knees, trying to summon the energy for a plan of action. Just then, the dense oleander next to the berry bed rustled, and a raccoon's pointy nose emerged. It paused, eyeing Beth with its beady black eyes.

Startled, Beth stared back. "Shoo!" she called out, realizing the raccoon had no intention of leaving. "You're not one of those rabid ones, are you?"

The raccoon, unperturbed, took a few more steps toward her. Keeping its eyes on Beth, it plucked a shiny, ripe strawberry from the nearest plant. Calmly, it turned and disappeared back into the oleander, the strawberry clutched in its mouth.

"Okay," Beth muttered, rising to her feet. The small wound on her finger throbbed. She liked roses and raccoons well enough, but she drew the line at bloody pricks and bold daylight intruders. "All right, fine," she declared to the flowers, the sea, and the empty air. "I'll hire a gardener. And someone for the house."

She was just about to head inside for a cup of coffee when her cell phone rang. Lately, she'd been getting a lot of spam calls, but she always answered anyway. If she didn't, she'd obsess over the missed call, wondering who it might have been.

With a sigh, she reached for her phone, not bothering to check the caller ID. "Yes? This is Elizabeth Thompson."

A male voice, smooth and professional, replied. "Good morning, Beth. This is James Cartwright from Cartwright & Associates. How are you today?"

Beth sat back down, her mind racing. She hadn't spoken to the lawyer who handled Ben's will in over a year. As far as she knew, all the business between them had been settled. "Oh, hello, Mr. Cartwright. I'm doing well, thank you. How can I help you?"

"I'm calling regarding some important developments in your late husband's estate. We recently finalized an expedited probate process for a will."

Beth frowned, confused. "Is this about Ben's will?" She'd been sure everything had been taken care of. It had been a simple estate—no children, no other heirs. She was the sole beneficiary, and everything had passed to her smoothly.

"This is not about Ben's will" James Cartwright said. "In this case, it's Ben who would have been the beneficiary. Since he has passed on, this clause has significant implications for you, Beth."

"Are you saying I've inherited something?"

"Yes, that's right," the lawyer said, a hint of a smile in his voice. "You've inherited something."

Beth pressed a hand to her forehead. "From whom?" Both her and Ben's parents had passed long ago. As far as she knew, there were no aunts or uncles who might leave something to her, someone who was already well-off.

There was a rustling of papers. "A woman named Margaret Porter. Do you know her?"

"No." Beth frowned. "I've never heard the name. Who was she?"

"I can't tell you much more than that she lived in Bay Harbor, Maine."

"But I don't know a Margaret Porter from Bay Harbor, Maine. There must be a mistake."

James Cartwright cleared his throat delicately. "I believe it's likely your husband knew her."

"Oh." Beth rocked back in surprise. "Oh. Right."

"Do you think you could come to the office in San Francisco at your earliest convenience? Or we can handle this online if you prefer," he said, his tone more formal now.

It took Beth a moment to gather her thoughts. For all she knew, Margaret Porter was just another architect Ben had worked with. Maybe she'd left him blueprint plans or a miniature model of a house they'd collaborated on? "Is it worth my time?"

"It's up to you, really."

"Then I suppose I'd better get this over with," she said, noting the slight tremble in her voice. "Yes, I'd prefer to do this in person. I'll be there this afternoon."

"Shall we say 3 p.m.? I have appointments before and after, but there was a cancellation." More paper rustled.

Beth glanced at the clock. It would be tight, but she could make it to San Francisco by then. "Yes, 3 o'clock is fine."

"Excellent. Well, thank you, and—"

"What is it?" Beth interrupted, suddenly too flustered to stand the suspense. "What has Margaret Porter left my husband?"

"Oh. Uh…" The lawyer hesitated. "I believe it's a beach house," he finally said, the sound of a keyboard clacking in the background. "Yes, it's a small beach house."

"In Maine?" Beth could hardly believe it. Why had a strange woman left Ben a house?

"I'm sorry for the confusion, Beth. Not in Maine, even though that's where the owner lived. The house is actually in Mendocino Beach, not far from your residence if your address is still the same."

"A house around the corner?"

"Yes, and I'm not certain of its condition."

CHAPTER 2

That's quite the story, Beth!" Hannah stacked the books on the counter and tucked a stray curl behind her ear. The bookstore was closed, and the evening settling over the streets of Mendocino Beach cast a velvety-plum light into the old bookstore, giving the tall wooden shelves a lavender glow. The warmth of the day slipped away, replaced by the cool, salt-tinged breeze from the ocean, which seemed to whisper secrets into the dim, cozy space.

She lingered for a moment, feeling the quietude of the bookstore, the familiar scent of old paper and ink wrapping around her like a soft blanket. This place had become her refuge, a sanctuary amid the chaos her divorce had caused.

But it wasn't only her own life in upheaval, it seemed.

"You inherited a beach house?" Hannah asked, making sure she'd heard right, turning back to Beth, one of her two best friends in town. It was hard to believe anyone would have such an unexpected windfall. Even in a small town like Mendocino Beach, coastal property wasn't cheap. Except for a few tucked-away million-dollar houses that seemed to change ownership every few years, families that were lucky enough to own seaside property tended to hold on to their homes.

Beth nodded, looking more tired than usual, the city's bustle still clinging to her in the form of a slight sheen of sweat. "That's what the lawyer said. I have the deed. It's crazy. I know."

"Let me see."

Beth readily pulled the papers from their yellow manila folder, sliding them across the wooden counter toward her friend. "There's the address." She pointed.

"Unbelievable. Congrats, my dear!" Hannah picked up the documents and scanned them. She knew the value of such a property, having watched the market for at least twenty years before her mother's old home had come back on the market. She'd talked Evan into buying it, grateful for her good luck. And while she'd lost her husband in the process—moving prompted Evan to finally come forward about his second family with Alli and baby Tommy—she'd gained sole ownership of her mother's house and the love of a much better man. Alex had loved her since they'd been in school together. At Hannah's lowest point, just after Evan announced he wanted a divorce and the house, Alex offered her refuge in the little bookstore he'd inherited from his father.

But soon after they'd decided to give things a go, Alex had to leave again. Officially, he was helping a friend in need. But when he'd told her that, he'd held her gaze in a peculiar way, letting her know there was more going on. Alex had never been one to talk about his past in the military, but every so often, a shadow would pass over his face, a look that told her there were things he couldn't say. This time, that shadow had lingered just a little too long when he'd mentioned helping a 'friend.'

During her sleepless nights, Hannah had come to a conclusion—either Alex's friend was an A-list celebrity who'd made Alex sign a non-disclosure form, or he'd been roped into a top-secret military mission.

Given his general lack of celebrity friends and evident background in the military, Hannah tended toward the latter. But she kept it to herself. If it was so secret that he couldn't tell her, she wasn't going to speculate.

But now it'd been almost four weeks since they last talked, and even though the coffee and cinnamon rolls he'd promised her still magically appeared at her doorstep every morning, Hannah knew it wasn't Alex who delivered them. The familiar warmth of the cinnamon rolls was beginning to lose its comfort. Her faith in him was starting to get just a little wobbly around the edges. The quiet unease gnawed at her insides with tiny yet pointy teeth.

Her ex-husband Evan's massive betrayal of her trust still loomed large in Hannah's mind. The only reason she wasn't frantic yet was that if it were another woman, Alex would not have held her gaze to communicate...something.

She trusted Alex; she really did. But Evan's betrayal had left scars—deep ones—and with every day Alex stayed away, more doubt crept in, whispering that maybe she was about to be blindsided again.

Hannah set the documents back on the folder and smoothed them. "Looks legit, Beth."

"I truly, legally did inherit a whole beach house." Beth sounded the words out as if she still couldn't believe them. "Oceanfront and all."

"Good for you." Smiling, Hannah looked up. "Let me guess...it feels weird since you didn't know the woman?"

"Absolutely." Beth slipped the folder back into her bag. "I haven't even looked at the house yet. I came straight to the bookstore. I just needed to talk about this with someone."

"Of course. I get it." Hannah studied her friend's face, recognizing the telltale signs of exhaustion, not just from the trip but from whatever emotional turmoil this unexpected inheritance had stirred up. Beth had been there for her when Evan's lies shattered her world, staying with her through the worst, even when words felt useless. Now, it was Hannah's turn to be that steady presence, offering her company and understanding.

Alex had asked her to take over the bookstore while he was gone. Since Hannah was a trained librarian who loved nothing better than books, she was happy with the task. But friends came first. Sorting the new books into the shelves could wait until the next day.

"Let's close the store," Hannah said gently. "It's too dark to properly admire your new house. Let's go have dinner and talk."

"I'd like that," Beth admitted, looking up with a small, weary smile. "I have to tell you, Hannah—I'm not looking forward to a long night of wondering who this woman was."

Hannah raised her eyebrows in understanding. She'd just gotten past the hideous shock of her ex's revelations and the sleepless nights. Even if the light on the other side of the tunnel turned out to be so much brighter—the tunnel was no fun. No fun whatsoever.

She slipped her phone and keys in her slouchy purse and slung it over her shoulder. "Italian?"

Suddenly, Beth looked uncomfortable. "Um," she said, tapping a finger against her lower lip. "Maybe not tonight. I've eaten a lot of Italian food lately."

"Hm-mm," Hannah hummed, just now remembering that Beth seemed to like a certain Italian restaurant. Or rather, the owner. Beth didn't admit it, but Hannah and Sara, their common friend, had both noted the light in Beth's eyes when he came to their table, telling them exactly what wine he'd chosen for Beth and why. "Then what? Greek?"

"I don't know."

"Thai?" Hannah smiled.

"Um..."

"How about you come to my house? I baked sourdough bread this morning. We can have bread and honey from the farmers market, and maybe a nice cup of peppermint tea. I grow it in the garden, and it makes the best tea in the world."

Beth smiled back, the tension easing slightly from her face. "The best tea in the world? Well then, how can I say no? I'd like that."

Hannah slipped her arm through that of her friend, and together, they left the store through the back. Under the stairs leading to the apartment over the bookstore, she suddenly stopped and leaned forward.

CHAPTER 3

"Alli?" Hannah called out, craning her neck to look up the staircase. A moment later, the door above opened.

Alli appeared, baby Tommy sleeping in the sling she carried across her chest. "Hey, Hannah. Hey, Beth."

"I'm leaving for today, Alli." Hannah smiled up at the young woman. "How's little Tommy?"

Alli had been due with Evan's baby before finding out Evan was already married. She left him right away. By accident more than design, she and Hannah eventually became friends, the two women bonding over the baby as much as their shared betrayal. Evan, meanwhile, had to give back Hannah's house and return to his old job inland.

"Tommy is good." Alli smiled back, her eyes softening as she looked down at the baby's head. "He slept through the night last night, and we had a great time at the beach earlier. He's all tuckered out."

Hannah nodded, knowing that Alli must be as tuckered out as little Tommy. "Do you need anything? I'm going to the market before coming here tomorrow."

Alli thought for a moment. "Would you mind getting me a jar of that blueberry jam?" she asked finally. "And bagels?"

"Of course. Do you need diapers?"

"I do need diapers," Alli admitted, a bit of color rising to her cheeks. "Are you sure it's not too much?"

"My pleasure, my dear. If you like, come over tomorrow morning. You can use the washing machine, and we'll have breakfast together. Maybe you can go have a nice swim while I get in some baby time. Oh, and Sara has the day off tomorrow and wants to take Tommy for a nice, long walk in the afternoon. She's going to text you."

"That's great. Thank you, Hannah. I'd like to come over, but now I'm going to bed. I'm pooped, and Tommy is settling down nicely. Who knows, maybe I'll get lucky again. Bye, you two." Alli waved, and then she went back into the cute little apartment over the old bookstore and closed the door.

After driving to Hannah's house, they parked at the curb and got out. "Your front yard is a riot of flowers," Beth noted as they walked to the front door through a sea of daisies and echinacea, brown-eyed Susan and daylilies, purple lavender and spotted lungwort. "I wish my garden would look like this."

"It needs a lot of work," Hannah said, regarding her little kingdom fondly. The soft evening light dipped everything in a soft blue, and the light she'd forgotten to switch off in the kitchen cast a warm, inviting glow from the windows. "But I enjoy it. Don't you? You have a big yard."

"It's just too much," Beth admitted with a hint of frustration. "I don't have green thumbs like Ben did, and I don't even know where to start."

"Do you want me to help you?" Hannah pulled out her key to unlock the door.

"Thanks, that's nice of you, but no. I'll hire someone."

Hannah pushed the door open and gestured for her friend to go ahead. "Frankly? With the size of your property, hiring sounds expensive."

Beth walked into the living room and dropped her purse on the sofa. "I know. That's not even all of it. I need someone to help with the house. Not cleaning as much as work on the house itself. I noticed the wood of the window frames is beginning to crack, and I think there may be a damp spot on one of the bedroom ceilings. The septic needs to be pumped, and there are a hundred more things I'm pretty sure need looking at. It's like everything's decided to fall apart at once."

"Oh dear." Hannah walked through to the kitchen and threw open the window and door to the garden. The property was situated on a bluff, and beyond her flower beds and peach trees and rhododendrons lay the Pacific Ocean. During the day, the water glittered and shone in the sun like a precious jewel, but under the rising moon, the sea spread like a soft, dark, twinkling cloud below. Hannah flipped the switch for the chains of tiny lights she'd spun around the patio, and they flickered on. Fireflies danced closer, drawn to the twinkling lights, and somewhere near the rocks, a sleepy gull cawed in protest. The warm scents of lavender and thyme drifted in the warm air.

For a moment, Hannah closed her eyes and, leaning against the door jamb, drew a deep breath of the fragrant, salty air, drawing it not only in her lungs but her entire being.

It had been a rocky, winding path to get to this perfect moment. Gratitude flooded her, filling her like the tide fills the coastal caves: quickly, completely, and with a force stronger than the water itself.

Smiling, Hannah exhaled and blinked.

Unlike Beth's architectural gem, her little seaside cottage was the perfect size. It was easy enough to keep things in order. There was plenty of space for herself and even a couple of spare bedrooms for guests upstairs.

Beth followed her and took in the view with a smile. "This is so beautiful. How do you do it?"

"I make fairy lights a priority," Hannah said, setting the kettle onto the stove to boil before stepping outside to pick some peppermint leaves. "And I love my garden. Sometimes I think I'm not just growing flowers—I'm growing memories. Every plant has its own story."

Beth sighed as she took the leaves and washed them before she sat at the wooden kitchen table Hannah's mother had sanded and painted herself. "Maybe that's my problem. I'm boring. I don't have any stories to tell."

"Aww, come now, cheer up, buttercup." Hannah brought the bread, butter, and honey and placed them on the table. "You just inherited a secret beach house! How's that for a story?"

The kettle whistled, and Hannah poured hot water over the fresh peppermint leaves she'd placed in a clay teapot. The rich, earthy scent filled the kitchen, and Beth inhaled deeply, closing her eyes.

"Why do you think Margaret Porter left Ben the house?" Hannah asked softly, slicing the freshly baked bread on a wooden board.

Beth opened her eyes, a cloud of confusion passing over her face. "I honestly have no idea. Ben never mentioned her, and she wasn't in his contacts on his phone when I checked before going to the lawyer. It's just so strange, Hannah." She rose to pour them each a cup of fragrant tea before she sat again.

Hannah spread honey on a slice of her soft, fluffy sourdough bread and passed it to Beth. "There must be a reason, something that connects her to Ben, or maybe even to you."

Beth took the bread but didn't eat it right away. Instead, she looked out the open window at the darkening summer sky, the waves crashing softly against the shore below. "I keep thinking about that, but I can't come up with anything."

Hannah reached across the table and squeezed her friend's hand. "We'll figure it out, Beth. You're not alone in this."

Beth exhaled, and then she finally took a bite of the bread, the sweetness of the honey making her smile despite her worries. "Thank you, Hannah. I don't know what I'd do without you."

Hannah smiled back, feeling a deep sense of gratitude for friendships that weathered any storm. "You'd do just fine. But I'm glad I'm here anyway."

They finished their bread and honey and went to sit outside.

"Have you so much as driven by the cottage?"

"Nope." Beth went back inside, and Hannah heard her open and close the kitchen cabinets before she returned with a bottle of wine and glasses. Her hand trembled a little as she tried to stab the tip of the corkscrew into the cork.

"Let me do it." Hannah took the corkscrew from Beth and twisted it into the cork herself. The wine was from the winery in Mendocino Cove, a merlot so soft and sweet she'd bought three bottles. She plopped the cork and filled the two long-stemmed glasses, then went into the living room and pulled two cashmere shawls off the sofa before returning to the patio.

She handed one to Beth and sat in the crackling wicker set that had been a housewarming gift, arranging her featherlight shawl over her shoulders.

Mendocino nights could cool quickly, and even though the air was still warm and the sea breeze kept the mosquitoes away, Hannah liked to have a little something over her arms out here at night. The cashmere shawls were soft like cobwebs, cool when the air was warm and warm when the night cooled.

"Mmm." With a sigh, Beth sank into a wicker chair. The rattan crackled softly as she, too, cuddled into the wool. "This is nice."

"Cheers. Congratulations again on your inheritance." Hannah lifted her glass. Beth followed her example but then hesitated.

"Seriously, though," she said in a low voice. "Why would a woman from Maine leave something as valuable as a seaside house to my husband?"

Hannah leaned over and clinked her glass against Beth's. She didn't want to think about the possibility of more betrayal and heartbreak. But she could see that her friend needed to talk about it. "I don't know, my dear," she said lightly and tasted her wine. "Maybe they were friends?"

"Obviously, they were." Beth took a deep drink. "The question is, Hannah—were they more than that? None of my friends ever left me a whole house."

"Yeah," Hannah admitted. "I know. Maybe they were related? A forgotten great-aunt?"

Beth shook her head, gazing distractedly at the soft peace of the night garden. "We did our family tree to hang it on the wall. Everyone is accounted for. She can't be a relative."

"Maybe an admirer?" Hannah plucked a sprig of lavender from a nearby terracotta pot, crushing its fragrant flowers between her fingers. "In a professional context, I mean," she added. "A lover of architecture."

"Maybe," Beth murmured and lifted the bottle, hovering its mouth over the glass. "Do you have a spare toothbrush? Can I spend the night?"

Hannah smiled. "Yes, I have, and of course you can. I'd like that. But do you maybe want a little bit of cheese to go with that?"

"Yes, please." Beth poured the velvety wine, the dark garnet color shimmering in the twinkling lights. "Actually, I'd like a lot of cheese."

Hannah nodded and rose to go into the kitchen. She'd definitely had nights where she needed a friend, a glass or two of sweet merlot, and a block of cheese to hang on. "You know, it'll be okay," she said. "It's Ben, isn't it? You love him."

"I did love him," Beth repeated. "More than any-one."

Hannah didn't point out the subtle difference be-tween the past and present tense they'd each used in their sentences. "It'll be okay," she murmured again, hoping it was true. "Let's go admire your new house tomorrow. Can we get inside?"

"I have the key," Beth confirmed. She sounded dis-tracted, her fingers nervously curling and uncurling around the stem of her glass.

Hannah wanted to say something more. Something comforting, something smart, something that reassured Beth her husband had been as faithful as Beth herself. But no words came to mind, and so Hannah simply went to load a board full of mellow cheese and savory salami, sweet grapes and briny olives, and the dark chocolate with roasted hazelnuts that was reserved for nights full of doubts and uncertainty.

CHAPTER 4

B eth parked at the curb and double-checked the house number. "This is it, girls," she said, her voice tight with unease. She'd not slept well at all, even though the bed in Hannah's guest room had been soft and comfortable, and the lavender night breeze drifting in through the open window was calming and sweet. But thoughts of Margaret and Ben had kept her awake, staring at the dark ceiling.

How had he never mentioned the woman?

Sara leaned across to peer out the window. "I didn't even know there was a beach here," she said. "I've lived in this town for ages, and I've never been down this road."

"Probably because it's a dead end," Hannah said from the back seat, cracking open her door. "This is the last house on the street. Unless you're visiting a neighbor, there's no reason to come this far."

"Come on, Beth," Sara said, laughter in her voice. "Cheer up! I'd be over the moon if I'd inherited a house like this."

Beth forced a smile, though her insides were knotted with a mix of emotions. Sara's difficult marriage made it clear she might dream of a small seaside escape like this. "Yes," Beth said, trying to sound upbeat. "Let's go see what I've got here."

They stepped out of the car into the hot July sunshine, crossing the gentle slope of the street.

"Whoa," Sara exclaimed, stopping in the front yard. "There's a beach, all right! You can't see it from the road."

"This is lovely," Hannah said, touching Beth's arm gently. "It needs work, but what a beautiful property."

"Yeah." Sara's voice was soft, almost reverent. "You can't buy a house like this for gold or good words these days, Beth. People just don't give them up. It must be worth a fortune."

Beth nodded, surprised. She hadn't expected this fairytale cottage nestled in a wild garden like a forgotten pearl, overlooking a small cove with a beach like a golden crescent moon.

"It's been a while since anyone lived here," Sara observed. Beth silently agreed. Despite its obvious charm, the little house had an air of abandonment. Yet, Beth felt enchanted.

"And? What do you think, you lucky duck?" Hannah was looking at her with a smile.

Beth's smile back felt more genuine now that she didn't have to pretend to like what she saw. "We should go in." Pushing aside the mystery of the situation for now, she led the way through the overgrown front yard to the cottage. The weathered wood shingles and white accent trims, the charmingly pitched roof and dormer windows reminded Beth of a long-ago trip she and Ben had taken to Nantucket. "What's this style of house called?"

"I believe it's a Cape Cod cottage," Sara said behind her.

"Look, Beth." Hannah had stepped onto the front porch and pushed aside a curtain of kudzu vines to reveal a wooden swing. "You need to cut this back ASAP. It's about to choke the roses."

Beth looked up. The porch railings were indeed draped with climbing roses. But unlike the red roses in her garden at home, the full blossoms tumbling from the posts and railing here were snowy white, peach, and bright, cheerful shades of yellow.

Sara squinted critically at the other plants around them. "There's a stone path," she said, pointing. "It's totally overgrown, but it should be easy enough to clean up. And look at those blue hydrangeas. A bit of pruning and fertilizer, and they'll give you tons of flowers."

"Try the key," Hannah said eagerly. "I need to look inside."

Beth stepped up to the door and pushed the key into the lock. It turned easily and without protest, as if the house had been waiting for her all along. Taking a deep breath, she stepped inside, her friends close behind.

Slowly, they wandered through the sun-filled cottage.

The living room was bright and inviting, with a cozy a stone fireplace. The walls were painted a soft, beachy blue, and the dusty hardwood floors gleamed with a warm sheen. Overstuffed armchairs and a sofa in shades of cream looked faded but soft and comfy, and wide glass French doors offered a stunning view of the ocean.

The kitchen was rustic, with white cabinets, butcher-block countertops, and a farmhouse sink. "Look at this," Sara said, picking up a blue-and-white china dish from an open shelf. "I think you've inherited not just the house, but everything in it."

"I think you're right," Beth replied, lifting a mason jar filled with shriveled, dried beans before setting it back on the counter. "It feels like someone just walked out, locked up, and forgot all about it." She moved to the small breakfast nook with a round table and mismatched chairs by a large window. Leaning across, she unlocked the window and pushed it open, filling the room with the clean sea breeze. The glass panes swung out easily, brushing the tall tips of hollyhock and foxglove that grew below.

"Picture yourself having morning coffee here," Hannah said softly beside her. "It's so pretty!"

"Hmm." Beth tried not to, but the images came unbidden. She was standing in her fluffy cream-colored morning robe by the open window, a steaming cup of milky coffee in her hand, gazing out at the half-moon beach and the ocean sparkling in the morning sun...

"Let's go upstairs!" Sara called from the other end of the house, startling Beth from the pleasant thoughts. Soon, they converged at the bottom of the staircase.

Upstairs, they found four cozy bedrooms. Two were empty except for beds covered with pretty, pale floral bedspreads. The third was a proper guest room with an inviting yellow-quilted bed, an antique dresser, and a matching armoire in soft pine wood. But the built-in bookshelf was empty, and the walls were bare of pictures or decor.

The master bedroom, on the other hand, looked as if someone had just stepped out for a moment. The bookshelves were crammed full of books, and pretty, framed aquarelles of seascapes brightened the white walls. There was a four-poster bed draped with airy white curtains in dire need of dusting and French doors that opened onto a private balcony. The adjacent bathroom had a porcelain clawfoot tub, a mosaic floor of white and light-green subway tiles, a pedestal sink, and a natural-edge wooden mirror. On a low bamboo stool sat a folded towel, and when Sara opened the built-in closet, they found more towels, linens, and a row of tiny, sample-size perfume bottles.

Beth picked one up, studying the label: Bois de Portugal. Expensive, the perfume of royalty. And, coincidentally, Ben's favorite fragrance. She could smell the faint scent lingering in the bottle. Or was it her imagination? Her stomach twisted with anxiety. She set the tiny bottle back and closed the cabinet, her thoughts swirling. Suddenly, she needed to escape the house.

"Let's go," she said curtly and turned, hearing her friends follow her. The French doors in the living room led out onto a large wooden deck, partially shaded by a pergola entwined with wisteria and the ever-invasive kudzu vine. The remnants of old string lights criss-crossed above their heads, and a few stone steps led to a narrow, sandy path winding its way from the backyard down to the beach.

"I'd give my left arm to inherit a house like this," Sara said, her voice filled with longing. "I'm so jealous I can barely breathe."

"Relax," Beth said, patting Sara's back. "I already have a house—if you want, you can move in here."

"Wish I could take you up on that." Sara bumped her hip lightly into Beth's, lifting her hand and wiggling the finger wearing her wedding band. "Maybe once the kids graduate high school, if Andy doesn't mind."

"About that," Hannah said, linking her arm through Beth's and then through Sara's, gently pushing toward the inviting beach path. "I think you should consider moving in here yourself, Beth."

"It's crossed my mind," Beth admitted. "But I could never."

"Why not?" Hannah encouraged her. "You just told me last night that your house feels too big and is too much work. This cottage is the perfect size for some-one like you, and it's close to Sara and me and every-thing Mendocino Beach has to offer."

"That's true," Sara said wistfully. "Once you clean her up, the cottage is just about perfect. You even have your own beach, Beth. What more could you want?"

Beth stopped at the edge of the path where it met the beach. She let go of Hannah's arm and kicked off her espadrilles, stepping into the warm, sun-kissed sand. Everything her friends said was true. She knew it.

It was the perfect place. But...

"Ben built our house," she said softly. "Besides, I need to know who Margaret was. Why would she leave something like this to my husband?" She turned to gaze out at the sea. "He never once mentioned her to me." The words that came next were hard, but she needed to say them out loud. "Did Ben and Margaret have an affair? Was Margaret in love with my husband? Is that why she left him this cottage?"

CHAPTER 5

B eth stood in the sun-drenched kitchen, inhaling the warm scent of fresh coffee as she took in the inviting space.

She still wondered about Ben's relationship to Margaret. But despite the worry gnawing at her heart, she couldn't help but return to the sea every day. Like a magnet, the cottage drew her back as soon as she left.

At first, Beth simply wandered through the rooms, occasionally sitting down to soak in the atmosphere and becoming more and more familiar with the space. After a while, it seemed as if the house adapted to her, fitting itself around Beth and her ways.

On the fifth day, Beth placed a vase of white hydrangeas on the table in the breakfast nook, drank a cup of coffee with cream, and ate two raspberry donuts by the open window. Afterward, she went upstairs, stripped the linens and curtains from the four-poster bed, and washed them in the old washing machine that stood in the pantry.

That act set off an avalanche. Once she started, Beth couldn't stop cleaning her little house. It wasn't as fancy or modern as the home she and Ben had shared, but it possessed a charm that took Beth some time and consideration to define. Eventually, she settled on 'just right.'

She was in her Goldilocks zone. Everything seemed just right—not too large, not too small for a woman with a small handful of good friends. It felt just exactly as safe as Beth wanted to be, without isolating her from the world. It looked charming but not cutesy. The deck had the perfect size for entertaining, and the garden sprawled just enough to maintain without getting frustrated. The entire house felt simply just right.

And when Beth stayed until the evening and sat in the kitchen, or the garden, or the living room, or even found a reason to be upstairs, she could almost hear the laughing echoes of family dinners and the sweet hum of late-night conversations. It felt like a place where memories could be made. It felt like new stories already waited in the sweetly scented, salty air.

"Time for a new chapter," she found herself whispering to the house, running her hand over the roughened edges of the countertop. "Okay, my friend. Let's give you a makeover."

Beth had always dreamed of renovating a house. But Ben had been the architect. Since he was always so sure of his vision, she'd been content to sit back and let him create.

Now, for the first time, she stepped into another space that felt just right: creating a home solely for herself. From the pictures on the walls to the lamps on the ceiling, from the rugs on the floor to the paint colors, Beth got to choose exactly what she liked.

She rolled up her sleeves and got to work, starting with the cabinets. With a screwdriver in hand, she started to remove the doors, each creak and groan of the old hinges resonating in the quiet.

Two hours later, the cabinets were bare. Beth stepped back, hands on her hips, and imagined the open shelving she planned to install. But first, the walls needed a fresh coat of paint. She chose a soft seafoam green that reminded her of the ocean, and when she dipped the roller into the paint tray and that first fresh streak appeared on the wall, a new sense of joy washed over her.

As the green paint rolled onto the walls, the room transformed. The color breathed new life into the space, making it feel even more airy and welcoming. "It's like a breath of fresh air," she said aloud, smiling. She liked how it sounded and said it again. Then, knowing she was alone in the house and not bothering anyone, she started to sing the words, as off-key and loud as she wanted, until she had to laugh at herself and stopped to sit on the stoop in the sun and drink a glass of iced peach tea with sugar.

The following day dawned bright and inviting as Hannah and Sara arrived, bringing an assortment of lush ferns, vibrant spider plants, cascading pothos, and graceful palms. Together, they potted these beauties in the pretty containers Beth had ordered online, arranging them in the rooms. While her friends continued working their magic with the plants on the patio, Beth turned her attention to the countertops.

With the assistance of a local carpenter, she meticulously measured and ordered redwood that would fit the space flawlessly. Donovan's Sawmill delivered quickly, and soon, the scent of freshly cut timber filled the house, mingling beautifully with the gentle sea breeze wafting through the open windows and doors.

Installing the countertops was no easy feat. They carefully maneuvered the heavy slabs into place, securing them with brackets and screws, then sanded the edges smooth and sealed the countertop.

Next came the backsplash for the deep farmhouse sink. Beth and Sara drove to the big home store in Maytown, where Beth chose glossy white subway tiles, thinking they would catch the light and add a touch of elegance. She spent hours meticulously placing each tile, spreading adhesive with a notched trowel, and pressing them into place. The repetitive motion felt meditative, and when she finally wiped away the excess grout and straightened her aching back, Beth felt a deep, new sense of satisfaction.

When everything else was done, Beth and Hannah hung the floating shelves the carpenter had made from leftover redwood and stocked them with vintage mason jars filled with oats, brown sugar, and coffee beans. She placed her favorite cookbooks alongside the jars, imagining the dinners she might cook for her friends. It felt cozier here than in the vast kitchen of marble and steel in her old house, especially at night. And with her friends living just a short walk away, it made perfect sense. It was just a skip and a hop to her friends' houses, sparing them the long drive. So there were plenty of good reasons to do it here...

Even if, of course, she still lived in Ben's house, not Margaret's cottage.

She stood in the middle of the living room, hands on her waist, mind churning with plans about restoring the old wood floor to its former glow and glory, when the doorbell rang.

Beth glanced over her shoulder; neither Hannah nor Sara would ring—they'd simply barge in, yelling that they'd arrived and for Beth to get down, or inside, or do whatever it was she had to do to come and meet them.

The bell rang again; maybe the cheerful cotton rug she'd ordered for the entryway had arrived. Pondering where she should place it, Beth went to open the door.

Standing outside was a man. Beth's eyes widened in surprise as she recognized the owner of the small Italian restaurant she liked so much. She didn't know much about him—not even his name. But he always knew her favorite dishes without asking and had once volunteered that he'd moved from Rome, Italy, to the States as a teenager. Beth was also aware that he was one of the most perfectly handsome men in, possibly, the world. She was a lot more aware of it than she should be...

His dark almond eyes blinked in surprise when he saw her, but then they lit up. "It's you," he said, running a hand through his dark hair, which just started to silver at the temples. "I noticed someone new moved into our quiet street. So, it is you. Then we are neighbors now." A smile warmed his voice, and he held out the small potted tree in his hands. "I brought you a gift, Beth."

"Thank you so much." Confused but pleased, Beth accepted the little tree with its glossy leaves. "That's very kind of you."

"It is an olive tree." The smile spread to his lips. He pointed at the olives growing between the leaves.

"Oh. Um." Beth cleared her throat. "I'm so sorry. I don't know your name."

"It's Matt." He bowed his head slightly.

"Matt?" She smiled. The name did not seem a great fit for the fiery dark eyes and Roman features.

He smiled back. "Well, really, it is Mateo. Mateo Leonardo Conti. But most people call me Matt."

"I like Mateo." Beth shifted the tree to one hand and held out the other. "Elizabeth Thompson, formally. It's nice to finally make your acquaintance."

He took her hand, and for a moment, she thought he was going to press a kiss on it. But then his grip on her hand subtly changed, and he simply shook before letting go. "I live in the house next to you." He gestured toward the neighboring home, only the top level visible behind the swell of a grassy dune. "If you need something, let me know."

"Thank you. Thanks very much." Beth felt her smile deepen. "I'm only renovating. I inherited the house recently."

"Ah." He nodded. "It stood empty for many years. Now I understand. So you are not going to live here then?"

Beth was about to agree—that she wasn't planning to live in the cottage. But then she looked down at her little olive tree and shrugged. "I'm renovating it," she repeated, evading the question. "It is a charming house, but it needs a fresh coat of paint."

The smile in his eyes darkened. "It is very charming. Well, you know where to find me if you want a hand." Again he inclined his head in greeting, then turned around and walked away slowly.

Watching Mateo leave, Beth moistened her lips. She wanted to call out, to ask him to come in for coffee.

But maybe that was too much. Maybe she wasn't ready to entertain handsome men with dark almond eyes and silver temples who brought gifts and knew how to cook—and how to quicken the beating of her heart.

CHAPTER 6

Lily pulled her suitcase from the trunk of the car and shaded her eyes against the afternoon sun. The cottage stood just as she remembered, though more ramshackle and overgrown than before. Sorrow pressed down on her as she stared at the dilapidated cottage, memories flooding back. It was ages since she'd last visited. Twenty years? She couldn't remember how old she'd been. Somewhere between five and ten years old. Eight, maybe. Eight was a long time ago.

She had no idea who lived here now.

Lily turned to the driver. "Hey—do you think you can wait a few minutes?" She dug a five-dollar note from her pocket and offered it.

He took it, glancing at his watch. "How long do you think?"

She shook her head, unsure. "I don't know. Five minutes? Ten?"

"Ten is okay," he said and leaned back in his seat, taking his cell phone from the dash holder. "Then I have to leave."

"Thanks." She straightened and gripped her suitcase. The ground was too sandy to use the wheels, but luckily it wasn't very heavy. She didn't own that much stuff. She crossed the empty street, hoping the circling gulls above wouldn't swoop down on her.

There was a car in the driveway and an open window with a gauzy white curtain fluttering in the breeze. Nervously brushing back her short blonde hair, Lily climbed the steps onto the front porch and knocked before she could lose her nerve.

"Just a moment!" a female voice called out inside. As promised, the door opened soon after.

For a strange moment of déjà vu, Lily blinked at the middle-aged woman standing before her in a dusty shirt and paint-splattered jeans. She felt as if she'd seen her before, that they knew each other, that they might have been friends. But as quickly as it came, the impression vanished, evaporating like a drop of salt water on a sun-warmed rock.

"Can I help you?" The woman smiled, lifting a quizzical eyebrow.

"Hi. Um, I'm sure this must seem a little strange." Lily's heart drummed with anxiety. "But I was wondering if you have a moment?"

"To do what?" Now the woman's eyes narrowed slightly as if she expected a sales pitch for an encyclopedia.

"This house used to belong to my grandma," Lily explained hastily. "And I just came to town for my mother's funeral. I was wondering—" She took a deep breath. "I know it's weird, but I need a place to stay for a few days. There aren't any hotels in town, so I thought

I'd ask if you might be willing to rent out a room?" She stopped, feeling too awkward to continue.

Embarrassed, Lily covered her forehead with a hand. "It sounded a lot saner in my head than it did when I said it out loud. I'm sorry," she said lamely, glancing back toward the street.

Her driver was still parked at the curb. She'd found a hotel in Mendocino Cove online. It would be inconvenient to drive back and forth all the time, but perhaps there was a bus. Or maybe the hotel owned a bike she could borrow.

The woman studied Lily, her blue eyes younger and more vulnerable than the rest of her guarded expression. "The house belonged to your grandparents? What's your name?"

"Lily," she replied. "Lily Porter."

"And your grandparents were...?"

"Darian and Debbie Porter," Lily said. "But Grandpa passed away before my birth. I only knew Grandma." Feeling a spark of hope, she looked up. "Did you know Debbie Porter by any chance?"

"No, I don't think so." The woman's face fell with disappointment, but then she composed herself. "Listen, I'm sorry to ask," she said, and Lily could see it was, in fact, difficult for her to form the words. "But you said your mother passed away. What was her name?"

"Margaret. But everyone called her Maggie, really." Lily couldn't help but smile softly at the thought. Mom had hated being called Margaret. *Feels like Ma is call-*

ing me to clean up my mess, she'd joked. But Lily's smile faded quickly as the weight of her loss settled back in.

"Your mom passed away recently?" the woman asked softly.

Lily nodded, pressing her lips together. "She did."

"Well..." The woman cast an assessing look over her shoulder into the house. "To be perfectly honest, the place needs a lot of work. I'm elbow-deep in cleaning and dusting. But if you don't mind the mess, come on in, honey. My friend just dropped off a cake and iced lemonade. At least you can sit down for a while and rest. I have a car, and if you want, I'll take you to the hotel in Mendocino Cove later. They're usually booked, but they'll make room for you."

"I'd love a glass of lemonade," Lily said, feeling relieved, shy, and disappointed all at the same time. "If you don't mind?"

The woman smiled that she did not, her guarded expression softening. "I'm Beth." She stepped aside to let Lily in. "Beth Thompson."

"Nice to meet you, Beth." Lily entered the house that she remembered from her childhood. When she turned to face her host, she saw that Beth was watching her with a curious expression. "It's very kind of you, letting me come in," Lily said, wondering whether she'd missed a social cue.

"Not at all. Nice to meet you too, Lily." Beth closed the door and waved for Lily to follow her.

Lily left her suitcase by the door, hurrying to catch up. In the living room, the sofa and couches stood shoved along the walls, a full, steaming bucket and wet mop stood by the fireplace, and the floor glistened from being washed, smelling of lemons and soap.

"Watch where you step!" Beth called, already in the kitchen. "It's slippery where it's wet; I think I poured too much soap in the water. We'll sit in the garden."

"Did you just move in?" Lily asked when she entered the room. The faded Formica countertops and yellow cabinets of her childhood were gone. Instead, there were gorgeous redwood countertops, the cabinets were painted in a soft, creamy white, and wide, gleaming floorboards of soft honey pine added a warm glow to the cozy space. Screwdrivers and other tools lay on the counter amid tote bags, rags, and bottles of cleaners and polish.

"I've been fixing the place up for the past few days." Beth opened the fridge. It, too, was new and had clearly recently been wiped, faintly smelling of the fresh peaches Lily spotted over Beth's shoulder in a polka-dotted bowl.

Beth took out a glass pitcher full of lemonade, ice cubes clinking as she handed it to Lily. "Would you mind bringing that out?" She nodded toward the deck overlooking the garden.

"Of course." Stepping out in the sun, Lily carried the pitcher out to the long, faded teak table. Now, this garden and this table, or one very much like it, she still remembered. Smiling at the memory, she set the pitcher down. They'd sat at this table for long, leisurely dinners with Grandma. Usually, there were at least a handful of friends and neighbors who joined them, though she couldn't remember names or faces.

Sometimes, Lily had been the only child, but often there were others too.

She recalled inviting them with shy smiles to join her in exploring the beach, searching for sea stars and sand dollars in the fading light, jumping from Grandma's rowboat into the freezing, knee-deep water, and hunting for crabs in the tide pools in the cliffs.

She inhaled deeply, drawing in that wild scent of kelp, bleached driftwood, sand, and salt. Suddenly, Lily realized that the beach held some of her happiest childhood memories. How had she forgotten this place?

"Have a seat," Beth said, placing a white tray on the table. It held glasses, napkins, plates, and a beautiful Bundt cake studded with plump blueberries and glazed with lemony icing. Lily's eyes were magically drawn to the golden, fragrant cake, making her feel like she was five again. But after traveling all day, she was both parched and starving.

"It looks wonderful." Smiling, Lily helped set the table. Even if she couldn't stay in her grandmother's house, the friendly welcome helped settle her nerves that were raw from the struggle of the last weeks. "Thank you, Beth," she said when the last napkin was folded and tucked under the plate. "I really didn't mean to intrude on your day like this. I don't know what I was thinking, knocking on your door. But I'm glad we get to do this."

Beth looked up, her eyes again searching Lily's face for something. Then she adjusted the placement of her glass. "No worries, honey. Your grandmother lived here; of course you'd come here first. Are you hungry?"

"I am," Lily admitted. "I haven't thought of food until now. But the cake smells delicious."

"Do you want something more than cake? I have plenty of venison stew with dumplings and lingonberry sauce left over from lunch. I could reheat it." Beth smiled. "Another friend dropped that off this morning."

"I wish I had friends who can cook!" Lily's mouth watered at the thought of a warm, savory stew. It sounded terribly good, but she didn't want to impose further, and the table was already set. Politely, she shook her head. "But the cake looks fantastic."

"Go ahead and pour the lemonade. I'll cut the cake." While Lily filled their glasses, Beth served them both luscious slices of the blueberry cake before taking a seat.

For a few moments, they chatted about the weather, the beach, the cake, the lemonade. The casual conversation eased Lily's shyness.

Then Beth set her fork down. "Listen, Lily, I have to ask you something," she said, her voice tentative.

"What's that?" Lily looked up, curious.

"The thing is—this house? It only recently came into my possession."

"Yes, I figured you just moved in." Lily wasn't sure where this was leading. "Because of the renovations."

"I didn't buy it. I inherited it."

"Oh?" Lily blinked. "Are you related to the previous owners?"

"No." Beth took a deep breath. "In fact, the previous owner—the one who left me this house—was Margaret Porter. Your mother."

Lily's eyes widened. "Really? I thought—well, I'd assumed Grandma sold it to pay for the senior living home. I guess not?"

Beth shrugged helplessly. "I don't know the details, honey."

"Mom never said, and I suppose I never asked, either." Lily felt her face flush warmly as the implications trickled through.

Not only had her mother never told her she still owned the house, but she'd left it to a perfect stranger. The lawyer never mentioned it to Lily, either. A sense of betrayal, or rather shame at having been excluded, flooded Lily. "I didn't know about this," she repeated quietly. "Why did Mom leave you my grandma's house?"

Beth frowned, clearly concerned at the show of emotions on Lily's face. "I'm sorry, honey," she murmured. "I'd tell you if I knew, but I honestly have no idea. Also, your mother didn't exactly leave it to me; she left it to my...my..." She paused, casting a doubtful look toward the sea as if seeking answers in the endless horizon.

"Your...what?" Lily braced herself, her heart pounding. Maybe there was a relative she didn't know about!

"My husband. Ben Thompson," Beth finished, her eyes returning to meet Lily's. "She left it to my husband, who has passed away. That's why it came to me." She sighed, her breath heavy with unspoken worry. "And I never heard about Margaret before all this."

"I never heard about your husband," Lily whispered. Everything in her quieted as a new sort of subdued shock spread through her muscles and bones, numbing the tips of her fingers and stiffening the set of her shoulders. "I don't know anyone named Ben. That's...weird."

"Yeah." Beth held her gaze. "It is, isn't it?"

"Um." Lily placed her elbows on the table and covered her face with her hands. She didn't want to think about this. She was exhausted from the trip, jittery from the sugary lemonade, and overwhelmed by grief. She had just gone through the harrowing process of transferring her mom's body back from Zimbabwe to California. She was maxed out. Spent.

"Are you all right, honey?"

Lily dropped her hands and looked at Beth.

Whatever was happening here, it wasn't this kind woman's fault. She needed to remember that in this sea of doubt and fatigue.

"I'm not really okay," she admitted with a laugh that sounded more like a hiccup or a sob. "It's been a lot since Mom died, you know? I'm not sure I can think about anything else. My mom was traveling the last few years of her life, and I was busy working. We fell out of touch. I didn't mean for it to happen. I didn't even realize it was happening. But it did. I thought we still had so much time to catch up."

"I'm very sorry." Beth's voice was filled with genuine compassion. "I'm really very sorry, my dear."

Lily swallowed hard. "Now I regret every call I missed, every call I didn't make." A lump rose in her throat, and she broke off, shaking her head to force it back down. "I'm sorry I don't know a Ben Thompson. I don't think I have any answers."

Beth reached out and placed a warm, reassuring hand on Lily's arm. Any other time, it might have made Lily smile. But now, it only reminded her of her mother, who used to comfort her the same way. It brought her loss into sharp, painful focus. Overwhelmed, she rested her arms on the table, hid her face in the crook of her elbow, and silently began to weep.

"Oh, dear," Beth said softly. Lily felt the bench shift as Beth sat beside her, gently stroking her hair. "Oh, sweetheart. I'm so terribly sorry for your loss."

CHAPTER 7

B eth watched as her young guest tried her best to regain composure. Lily's eyes reddened, and her chin dimpled with the effort of holding back tears, but Beth knew all too well that losing one's mother was one of life's most profound hardships.

She remembered the hollow feeling when her own mother had died just a year after her marriage to Ben, before their marriage solidified into a true partnership. It was as if the anchor that held her steady had been lifted, leaving her adrift in a vast, uncharted sea. The loss rippled through every aspect of her life, creating an emptiness nothing seemed to fill. When Ben died, the feelings returned. It wasn't the same, of course. But similar. She'd been adrift, quite literally wandering from room to room in the empty house, staring at the spots Ben would occupy that time of day.

"I think we need a pot of tea," she declared, pulling herself back to the task of comforting Lily. "You take your time out here. I'll be right back."

Taking the tray, she went into the kitchen to boil water and open the new box of vanilla tea she'd bought for the cottage that morning. After she poured cream into the pretty little blue pottery jug Hannah had gifted her, Beth put it, the matching bowl of brown sugar, the steaming teapot, and two large cups on the tray and carried it outside.

"I'm so sorry. I don't want to pull you down with me." Lily's hands trembled slightly as she clutched the teacup Beth handed her.

"Don't be sorry. What you're going through is hard, Lily," Beth said gently, opening the patio umbrella and sitting down. She passed the sugar and cream to Lily, glad to see she took a little of both. The calories would do her good—despite the tempting aroma of sweet lemon glaze, Lily barely touched her cake.

Beth had no children, but she'd always had a strong mothering instinct. If it were up to her, she'd make the girl eat a big bowl of hearty beef stew with homemade corn bread and ask her to cuddle up on the sofa with a blanket and a good book.

Beth looked down at the steaming cup in her own hands. "Losing a mother...it's like losing a part of yourself."

Lily nodded, tears welling up again. "I didn't act like it until it was too late, but she was my best friend," she whispered, her voice breaking. "I loved her so much. Now I just feel lost."

"I know." Beth reached across the table, taking Lily's hand. "When my mother passed, it was like the world shifted under my feet. Nothing felt stable anymore."

Lily looked up. "Does that feeling go away?"

Beth sighed. "It's more like you understand that the world is not stable. Our lives aren't like a single planet—more like a universe. The constellations of our planets and stars change. Gravity, time, birth and death, losing loved ones and finding kindred souls...they're like the laws of nature that apply. Whether we like it or not." She pulled her hand back and smiled. "Your universe rearranges itself; your stars and planets find a new pattern. The pain gets easier. But the grief never goes away."

"But the pain..." Lily's brow crinkled. "How do you get through that?"

"One day at a time," Beth replied softly. "I leaned on people who cared about me. I let myself cry." She leaned back, looking out over the flowers to the sea. "I'll never not miss her, and sometimes, it's still painful. But usually, I enjoy remembering her. I found ways to keep her memory alive in the things I do." She turned back to Lily, thinking how strange it was that she, of all people, was reassuring the young woman about her grief when she'd had such a hard time coming to terms with it. She was the last person qualified for that counsel.

Or maybe, it was the other way around. Exactly because it was so hard for her and she struggled with the same feelings Lily was going through.

"I think it's so sweet you keep her memory alive in things you do. I could do that too." As if to prove that last thought, Lily sniffled, a small smile touching her lips. "My mom loved gardening. She always said it was like painting with flowers."

Beth smiled back. "Are you a gardener too?"

Lily broke off a piece of her cake, crumbling it between her fingers and tasting a morsel before shaking her head. "What's the opposite color of green on the color wheel?"

"Red, I think."

"Then I have a red thumb. I love plants and gardens and all that, but as soon as I buy a plant, it starts to wilt on me."

Beth chuckled. "What do you do for a living?"

"I restore and upholster furniture. I have a small shop at the coast in Maine."

"That sounds wonderful. Do you enjoy it?"

"Yes," Lily said, her smile growing a bit. "I like working with my hands. I open the door to hear the ocean and the gulls while I work. It's peaceful, you know?"

"I can imagine." Beth sipped her tea, picturing the scene, hoping Lily would volunteer more information about herself. Beth had so many questions... But the girl was already barely coping with grief. This wasn't the time to delve deeper into the connection between Ben and Margaret.

"Mom wanted to be buried in Mendocino Beach," Lily said, her gaze drifting over the swaying flower heads to the sea. "I thought she should've picked somewhere closer to me so I could go visit the grave more often. But now I understand. It's really beautiful here. And who knows, maybe I'll move again."

"The funeral is still to come?" Beth asked gently. Since the estate had already been executed, she'd thought Margaret had died a while ago. "When did she pass away?"

"Two months ago, of a stroke. At least the doctors said she didn't suffer; it was all over in a flash." Lily sighed. "But the funeral has been delayed because she was traveling in Africa when it happened. It was really hard to communicate, and there was so much paperwork going back and forth, and then there were scheduling issues with the...um"—she swallowed, clearly reliving trauma before exhaling and continuing—"the transport back here."

Beth couldn't image how that would have felt. It was bad enough to settle things with the local funeral home. But to have to go through all that on top? "That must have been so difficult," was all she could think to say.

"Yeah, it was. But honestly, I'm not sure I'm ready for it all to be over. I've been avoiding it, in a way."

"Grieving takes time. There's no rush." Beth took a deep breath. She'd come to a decision a while ago, but now it was time to help her exhausted guest rest. "Listen, the bedrooms upstairs aren't ready—they still need dusting and mopping and fresh linens. But I can have a room ready for you tomorrow. You're welcome to stay here for as long as you need. It's easier for you to be closer to town, and you have fond memories of your family in this place. Maybe it'll help you feel less adrift." Beth picked another bloom from the potted lavender.

"And if you like, I can be one of the people you lean on."

Lily looked up. "Really? Even if you don't know me?"

"I know you a little bit." Beth smiled. "Definitely enough to want to help out."

"Thanks, Beth. I'd love to accept. It's a relief to have a place that reminds me of Mom to call home, even if it's just temporary."

"Then it's settled." Beth felt a mix of relief and a lingering sense of responsibility. "For tonight, let's get you settled at the hotel in the cove. You look exhausted."

"I am." Lily set her cup down. "I am so tired, Beth."

"Of course you are." Beth stood as well, gently placing an arm around her young guest's shoulders. "Let's grab your suitcase. I know the owner of the hotel; she'll take good care of you. They always reserve rooms for people returning home."

CHAPTER 8

The sun hung low in the azure sky of a warm June day as Hannah sat behind the bookstore counter, eyes fixed on a spreadsheet open on her laptop.

The bookstore made no profit. None, zilch, nada. Despite her best efforts, the bookstore was barely breaking even. They had sold only forty books in April, and the modest profits just covered the utilities. Alex had insisted on paying her a salary for managing the store in his absence, but she knew the finances couldn't sustain it.

"What's on your mind?" Sara asked, lounging in a comfy armchair in the corner. She was sketching patterns in her notebook, her sock-clad feet tucked beneath her.

Hannah sighed, turning to her friend. "I just don't understand how Alex keeps this place afloat. We should be drowning in debt, but somehow the doors are still open."

Sara shrugged, her pencil hovering over the paper. "He owns the building outright. If you don't pay rent, maybe it doesn't need much?"

"Maybe," Hannah said, unconvinced. "But it would be wonderful to order some new books. Most of our current stock has been picked over. The treasures are gone, and we're left with the leftovers."

"There are more books," Sara pointed out, nodding toward a stack of cardboard boxes.

"Those are secondhand donations. Not that I mind—I love giving old books a new life. But I was thinking about bringing in some bestsellers to attract more customers. If people knew they could get the latest releases here, they might choose us over on-line shopping."

"Are you sure?" Sara raised an eyebrow. "It's aw-fully convenient to buy online. Click a button, and voilà—a package arrives at your doorstep. A nice, thick bubble envelope with your new, shiny book."

Hannah shook her head. "I've had so many people stop me on the street and ask if we have book so and so in the store. And they are disappointed if we don't." She raked her fingers through her hair. "You know the number one predictor of human happiness?"

"The bottles of good chardonnay in one's fridge?" Sara closed her sketchbook, accepting that she had been properly roped into a conversation.

"No."

"Copious amounts of tiramisu?"

"Close, but also no. It's the tiny little human inter-actions over the day."

"Like with a baby?" Sara asked, smiling.

Hannah grinned. "Funny. No, like chatting with a cashier or buying a book in person. Those little moments make a difference. We can provide that here."

"A smile here and there, huh?" Sara nodded thoughtfully. "That does make a difference."

"Exactly. It does a body good, and none of us have enough of it."

Hannah clicked the spreadsheet shut and stood, stretching her arms. "You know what?" She leaned on the counter, pointing a finger at Sara. "We should organize a fundraiser for the bookstore."

"A fundraiser?" Sara fished her buzzing phone from her purse to check a message. "What kind of fundraiser?"

"I'm not sure yet," Hannah admitted with a shrug. "Maybe we need to convene the book club and brainstorm."

Sara put her phone back and patted her backpack. "I'm almost through the second chapter of the new book."

"You should be at chapter fifteen," Hannah said sternly. "We're meeting tomorrow night."

"So there's still time." Sara slung her bag over her shoulder. "It's an excellent idea to have a fundraiser for the store. Are you going to tell Alex?"

"He doesn't get my texts," Hannah said glumly. "I'll try again in two days."

"Are you going to tell him then?"

"No." Hannah tapped a finger to her lips. "Let's make it a surprise."

"Cool."

"The kids don't say cool anymore," Hannah said, watching her friend make her way toward the door. "I think it's squibbeldigoo now or something."

Sara reached for the handle, smiling as she looked back over her shoulder. "Ask the next kid who comes in to clarify," she recommended.

"Can't," Hannah sighed. "We don't have books for anyone younger than Gen X. I haven't seen a kid in these here lands since I arrived."

Sara laughed. "You really do need some new books then. You'll need at least a handful of millennials in the mix. I hear they are crazy for books."

"They are. And I intend to serve my community. By the way—how is Julian?" Hannah raised a quizzical eyebrow.

Julian Sterling was both a successful lawyer and Sara's boss. He was also, as far as Hannah could tell, smitten with her vivacious friend. But Sara was still married. Rather unhappily, Hannah knew, but Sara and Andy had two teenagers. One late book club meeting replete with red wine and cheese cubes, Sara had talked about her marital problems, in the end deciding to stick it out with Andy and get the marriage back on track for the sake of the kids.

"He's good." Sara turned so Hannah could no longer see her face. "He's doing his thing."

"And you?" Hannah asked gently. "How are you?"

Sara pushed open the door. "I'm good too," she said. Her voice was firm, but Hannah didn't miss the tiny wobble. "Bye, Hannah. See you tomorrow night."

"Bye," Hannah called after her as the door closed with a soft chime.

Left alone, Hannah fetched a box cutter from the drawer and approached the boxes in the corner. Kneeling down, she prepared to slice open the first box when a hand suddenly gripped her wrist. She gasped, dropping the cutter.

"Hannah!" Alex pulled her up and into his arms. "It's me! It's me."

"Alex! You—" Hannah's shock melted into joy. "What are you doing here?"

"I wanted to surprise you," he said, laughing. "When I saw you wielding that knife, it was too late to announce myself."

She playfully swatted his arm. "You nearly gave me a heart attack!"

He grinned, his irises like stars. "No knives allowed in the bookstore, remember? I had to disarm you."

"Well, mission accomplished." She tilted her head, a smile tugging at her lips. "I'm so glad you're back."

Without another word, Alex pulled her closer, wrapping his arms around her waist, his lips meeting hers in a long kiss. The world faded away as Hannah returned the kiss, letting herself sink into his embrace, hugging him to her.

"I missed you so much," he murmured, lightly resting his forehead against hers. "I couldn't stop thinking about you."

"I missed you too," she whispered, her hands trailing down to his shoulders. "How are you?"

"Better now that I'm back," he replied, his smile deepening. "Seeing you is exactly what I needed." He lifted her effortlessly, setting her on the counter.

"Alex!" Hannah laughed, her cheeks flushing. "Put me down!"

"You're right where I want you," he teased, lightly kissing her nose.

She shook her head, trying to appear stern when, really, all she wanted was to wrap her legs around him, pull him close, and kiss him like she meant it. "We're in a bookstore, in the middle of town. Anyone could walk in."

He glanced over his shoulder. "Door's locked, and the 'closed' sign is up. We're safe."

"You're impossible," she said, but her eyes betrayed her amusement.

He helped her off the counter, his hands lingering at her waist. "So, tell me about this fundraiser you mentioned."

Her eyes widened. "You heard that?"

"Couldn't help it," he admitted. "But I love the idea."

"I wanted it to be a surprise," she said, lightly punching his arm.

"Consider me pleasantly surprised," he replied, capturing her hand in his. "But enough about that. Have you eaten?"

She shook her head. "No, I was just thinking about grabbing something."

"Perfect. Let me take you to lunch. We have a lot to catch up on."

She smiled softly. "I'd like that. I have food in the fridge, in case you're tired from traveling."

"I'm not." His starry eyes were impossibly blue. "And if we stay here—I'm not sure I'll have the patience to do much talking."

She shook her head so she wouldn't have to laugh. "You're the worst. Or..." She took his hand, leaning into him. "Should I say the best? Because I actually am starving."

He kissed her again, pulling away with a groan. Now, Hannah couldn't stop herself from laughing. "You've really been gone for a long time, haven't you, soldier?"

He raised his eyebrows as he led her toward the door and opened it. "I've missed you for too long."

He opened the door for her. Smiling, Hannah passed by him, but when he locked up, she paused. "Where were you?" she whispered. "Where have you been, Alex?"

"I've been abroad, Hannah." His lids dropped when he turned to her, veiling his starry gaze. "I promise. You've always been the only one for me."

She stepped even closer. The ocean behind them rolled into the coast, and even if someone had stood with them, trying to listen in, they would not have heard a word. "Is it—officially a secret?"

A slow smile spread over his face as he held her gaze, confirming her suspicions. "The less you know, the safer you are." He brushed a stray curl behind her ear. "And keeping you safe is my number one priority."

Pressing her lips into a line, she nodded. "I trust you. I trust that you're keeping yourself safe. I hope you know that now that I found you, I can't lose you again."

"I'm just a small-town bookseller, Hannah. I'm safe."

Hannah could see how those eyes and that face might fool others. But she knew him better than that. She rose on her tiptoes to kiss him. "Just be sure to keep it that way, Mr. Bond," she whispered against his lips. "Because I love you."

CHAPTER 9

Beth stood in the pantry of her beach house, removing her old apron. She smoothed her hair and her long blue linen dress with its delicate white lace trim, casting a satisfied glance at the morning's handiwork.

The fresh scent of Sugar Lemon Kiss—the cheerful off-white paint she had chosen for its hint of sunny yellow—blended with the salty sea breeze. Happy with her progress, Beth inhaled deeply. She wiped the last of the paint from her hands and stepped into the kitchen.

Sara held up a steaming coffee pot, smiling. "Coffee's ready. Want some?"

"Sure." Beth tossed the kitchen towel aside and grabbed one of the meringues Sara had brought. "Thanks for these," she said, taking the mug Sara handed her with her free hand. "Wait—don't you have work?"

"Not on a Sunday." Sara filed her own mug and winked. "Must be nice not to have to worry about mundane things like the work week and paychecks." She sighed dramatically, vaguely waving her hand at the newly renovated kitchen. "And inheriting a beach house? So unfair."

"I agree." Beth raised her mug in a toast. "But the next best thing to inheriting a beach house is having a friend who inherits one. You're always welcome here, Sara. You can literally move in for the price of the utilities."

"Hmmm." Sara smiled, leading the way outside onto the deck. She tilted the patio umbrella to shield them from the sun.

Beth followed, carrying the tray of meringues. They were perfect—creamy white, light, and irresistibly fluffy. She settled into the chair next to Sara so they could both enjoy the view of swaying flowers and the ocean beyond. She took a sip of coffee, savoring the moment.

After a pause, Sara patted Beth's hand. "About that..."

"About what?" Beth asked, surprised. "Do you want to move in? How are things with Andy?"

Sara's tone was lighthearted, but there was a shadow in her eyes as she said, "It's so kind of you to offer, but I have a family. Who else would cook, drive, or buy groceries?" She tried to laugh it off, but the weight behind her words lingered.

"I know," Beth said gently. "Still, the offer stands."

Sara drew in a breath but then let it out with a shake of her head. "I want to talk about you."

"What about me?" Beth eyed her over the coffee mug.

Sara cleared her throat. "Have you thought more about moving in here?"

"I have a house." Beth's heart skipped a beat. Her pulse quickened, and a strange sense of panic stirred in her chest. Of course she had thought about it. Way too much, in fact... "I have a house," she repeated, a bit too sharply. "Ben built that house for me. I love it."

Sara reached out, placing a hand on her arm. "I know. We all know that. I didn't mean to upset you."

"I'm just getting a glass of water," Beth muttered, standing abruptly. "Do you want some?"

Sara gave her a sharp glance—nothing escaped her, with years of experience working for a top lawyer. "Sure, if it's not too much trouble."

Beth retreated into the house, glad for the excuse to gather her thoughts. It made so much sense to move into the beach house—the size was perfect, and it felt cozier than the sprawling home she and Ben had shared. She could entertain guests here, and there wouldn't be as much upkeep. Still...

Moving here meant leaving the house where she and Ben had lived together. Where every room whispered memories of their love. And their loss.

Beth filled the pitcher, her breath shallow. She'd told her friends that she wanted to move on, keeping them abreast of her little struggles and gains in her grieving process. But in the literal sense?

Was she ready to truly move on? She wanted to—Ben wouldn't have wanted her to cling to the past forever. The grief wouldn't vanish, but it didn't need to consume every part of her life. It would always have its place in her life. But not all places. Only its own. Beth wanted to give herself a second chance at happiness.

Sara wasn't attacking her; a discussion about moving presented no clear and present danger. What felt so dangerous to Beth was that she wanted to leave Ben's big, beautiful, empty house. She wanted to move here, into this adorable little cottage that seemed custom-ordered for a single woman in her best years.

But something still held her back. What if Ben and Margaret Porter...? The thought that they might have had an affair in this very house filled her with dread. No matter how charming the cottage, it would be tainted if betrayal lingered in its walls.

Steeling herself, Beth grabbed the pitcher and two glasses, then stepped back onto the deck.

Sara pushed her sunglasses onto her head, studying her friend. "You okay?"

Beth nodded, though her throat tightened. "It still gets to me, you know?"

"I know," Sara said gently. "Listen, it's okay. It takes time. People say it comes in waves. Tomorrow will be better."

Beth nodded. "Sometimes, I think it would be good to start over. I mean, really start over. Not like this, where I'm with one foot in the old world and one foot in the new." She drew a cloud into the condensation running down her glass. "I'm not quite there yet, though. I need time to get used to the idea."

"I get it. And hey, speaking of starting over...Andy just texted me to pick up the kid."

Beth raised an eyebrow. Shouldn't Andy handle that? He was home, after all. It seemed to her that on a weekend day, when Sara was visiting friends, Andy might pick up his child himself.

Sensing Beth's thoughts, Sara shrugged. "I'm closer, that's all." She stood up, hesitating briefly. "At some point, you stop asking, you know?"

Beth had never had to ask Ben repeatedly for anything. She felt a pang of sympathy for Sara's situation, unsure what to say. "I'm sorry."

Sara shrugged again. "Yeah."

That was all Sara said, and she didn't meet Beth's eye. They stood together, and Sara gave Beth a hug, holding on just a little longer than usual. "Don't work too hard, okay?"

"You too," Beth whispered. They walked to the door together.

As Sara opened it, she paused, glancing back with a smile. "Looks like you've got another visitor. Hey, I know him! Isn't he...?"

Beth rose on tiptoes to peer over Sara's shoulder. Mateo, carrying a foil-covered tray, was walking up the path. A faint blush warmed Beth's neck. "It's Mateo."

"Oh, that's right!" Sara tapped a finger to her lips, grinning. "The handsome guy from the restaurant you love so much."

Beth flushed deeper. Dark-haired and dark-eyed, dressed in jeans and a blue button-down with rolled-up sleeves that exposed a tantalizing glimpse of tan, muscular arms, there was no sense in denying the talented cook was extremely handsome. "He's just my neighbor."

Sara chuckled. "Just your neighbor, huh?" She smiled knowingly and walked out, stopping to exchange a few words with Mateo before heading to her car.

Mateo approached with a smile. "Your friend is very nice."

"She is," Beth replied, clearing her throat. "She had to go pick up her kid."

Mateo raised an eyebrow, his eyes warm. "No problem for me. I came to see you."

CHAPTER 10

"Oh." Beth moistened her lips nervously. "That's very nice of you."

Mateo inclined his head, acknowledging her words with a soft smile. "And I brought lunch. I thought, maybe she is renovating the house, working hard on a Sunday."

Beth smiled at his sweet, lilting Italian accent that lingered despite the years. "I did paint the kitchen pantry this morning."

"Ah, that's good. I like a beautiful pantry." His eyes crinkled into laugh lines. "I wanted to make sure you didn't forget to eat." He held out a tray wrapped in aluminum foil.

"Thank you." Beth took the tray; it was still warm, and it smelled delicious. She couldn't help but inhale deeply. The scent of freshly cooked pasta, rich and creamy, with hints of smoky pancetta and freshly grated parmigiano-reggiano teased her senses, despite having just eaten meringues. "What is it?" she asked, trying not to sound overly eager. Mateo's cooking really was her favorite.

"It is spaghetti carbonara." He made a hand gesture to indicate that she was very welcome. "It's nothing complicated, but it's a family recipe, passed down for generations."

Beth anticipated his next words: something about not wanting to intrude and that he'd be on his way. So, before he could, she stepped back, opening the door wider. "Would you like to join me for lunch?" she asked, surprising herself. "I want to make sure you don't forget to eat either."

The smile returned to his warm brown eyes. "I don't want to bother you," he said politely.

"No bother," Beth assured him. "In fact, I'd like the company. And I'd like to show you the house if you are interested. There's still a lot that needs to be done, but I started with the kitchen."

"Ah, the kitchen." Mateo stepped into the house, casually relieving her of the heavy tray. "It is always the heart of the house, no?"

"I think so." Smiling, Beth closed the door. "I don't know about other people, but whenever I have guests, they make a beeline for the kitchen. And I'm so fond of this one." She led the way through the hall and the sun-drenched living room, patting the new wooden counter in the kitchen when she reached it.

Mateo put the tray down and looked around, approval in his eyes. "It is very nice. It is warm and cozy and a good place for the family to gather."

Beth nodded as she imagined the pretty space filled with laughing relatives, chatting about kids and grandkids, sports and school and work, collectively arguing with that one weird uncle. "I wish I had a big, happy family like that," slipped from her lips before she knew it.

Mateo's gaze softened as if catching the hint of loneliness in her words. "My family is spread over several continents," he said, turning his attention to the wooden counter. "My parents lived in Mendocino until they retired, but they wanted to die in Rome." He shrugged that it was all good. "For my parents, it was their friends, you know. They still had so many good friends in Rome." He smiled. "Their friends and the fountains. My mother missed them."

"How are your parents?"

"Old." He grinned. "But I visit them often. I'll go before the summer ends."

Beth smiled. It was nice to hear how fond he was of his parents. "You must get along well."

"I love them very much, and they love me," Mateo replied, adding an expressive hand gesture. "Now, the carbonara is waiting. Where shall we eat?"

"We could eat outside if you like." She nodded at the door, and Mateo stepped outside. "Or inside. It's getting a little hot."

"You are right. Let's eat in the kitchen. One moment." He walked into the garden, picked a couple of the roses hidden by tumbling vines, and brought them into the kitchen. "Forgive me," he murmured, opening a cabinet to find a glass for the flowers. "It's a habit of mine to always have flowers on the table."

"That's a lovely habit," Beth said, admiring how the roses added warmth to the room. Feeling inspired—and perhaps a bit eager to put her best foot forward—she pulled out the china set she'd splurged on but never used. She'd brought it here because she and Ben had always used their wedding china in the old house.

Once the table was set, it looked beautiful. The delicate, hand-painted birds and vines on the china, the soft red roses, the sunlight filtering through the window, the mixing of elements, of wood and silver, crystal and light—all combined to create an inviting, intimate atmosphere.

"Please, take a seat," Mateo said and pulled out a chair for Beth to sit. "Allow me to serve you."

"Thank you." Beth watched as he expertly filled her glass with water and placed a generous serving of carbonara in front of her. The dish looked like a work of art: perfectly al dente spaghetti glistening with a golden, silky sauce, crisp pancetta scattered throughout, and a sprinkle of parsley for color.

"Enjoy, Beth," Mateo said, his eyes twinkling as he set her plate down.

Beth inhaled deeply, savoring the intoxicating aroma of the dish. She waited for him to join her and then twirled a forkful of pasta as best she could, tasting it with anticipation. When she took her first bite, the flavors burst in her mouth—creamy, smoky, and rich, with just the right amount of saltiness from the pancetta.

They chatted about the house, the neighborhood, and the beach. The conversation flowed easily, and Beth found herself relaxing in his presence. Every bite of the carbonara seemed to deepen the warmth she felt—not just physically but emotionally. Several times, she had to resist the urge to close her eyes or let out a satisfied sigh.

When she finally set her fork down, full but wanting more, Beth looked at Mateo, who was watching her with a satisfied smile. "It's incredible, Mateo. Truly. I've never had anything like it."

"I'm glad you enjoyed it," he said, his gaze steady. "Would you like more?"

"I would. But I can't. I was hoping to still take a beach walk before I have to go back to the house." She laughed. "My house, I mean. I mean, my real house." Beth took a deep breath. "I mean the house where I stay right now."

"You don't plan to live here?"

Beth hesitated, then changed the subject. She didn't want to talk about all that entailed... "Would you like to join me for the walk? I have another hour or so."

"You have someone waiting for you?" he asked, his tone casual but curious.

"No." Beth shook her head slowly. "My husband passed away a few years ago, and I don't have children."

He tilted his head. "And your parents?"

"They passed when I was in my thirties," Beth said, a hint of sadness in her voice. "But I have wonderful friends."

The breeze coming in through the window lifted her hair, and she shook it back. Mateo reached out, gently smoothing a lost strand back. "It is good to have friends," he said softly. "Better not to be lonely."

Beth's heart fluttered at his touch, and she blurted out, "I bet you're never lonely—with your restaurant and everything. You must always be busy."

"Busy and not being lonely are different," he pointed out and rose, taking their plates and putting them in the sink, running water into it. "I did not speak English when I first came to California, and my parents were always working."

"Oh. That must have been hard."

He glanced back at her, his eyes warm. "I know how loneliness feels, Bella. It can squeeze your heart until you can't breathe."

"It's not that bad," Beth replied quickly, embarrassed by her earlier admission of loneliness. "I keep busy. I'm in a book club."

"That helps." Mateo smiled, drying the plates. "Now, how about that beach walk? I can show you the best spot for sea glass."

Beth stood, smoothing her linen dress. "That sounds nice," she said, grateful for the change in topic. "I love sea glass. I used to have a collection as a girl, but I can't remember what happened to it."

"You can start over. It is a new beginning." Mateo joined her in the open door, offering his arm, and without hesitation, Beth accepted it. He started walking, leading her through the garden and down the sandy path toward the beach.

Mateo felt different from Ben—firmer, taller. Ben had been attractive, but an inch shorter than Beth and much thinner. She'd always felt too big beside him and avoided wearing heels. Mateo, on the other hand, was at least a head taller, with broad, strong arms, as if his work at the restaurant was more physically demanding than it appeared. And while Ben had always felt cold, Mateo's skin beneath her fingertips felt warm.

Beth was relieved when they reached the sand, as it gave her an excuse to release his arm and take off her sandals. She busied herself with the straps, hiding the confusion she was sure must be visible on her face.

How could she be so ridiculously attracted to Mateo? She barely knew the man.

Only an hour ago, she had nearly cried, missing Ben and wondering if he'd had an affair. And now, here she was, longing to feel Mateo's skin, imagining her fingers tracing the curve of his biceps, slipping through his thick black curls.

"Do you want help?" he asked when she took too long with the strap of her wedge sandal. "If you sit on the step, I can undo your strap."

"Oh, no—thanks. I've got it." Quickly, she slipped out of her sandals and held them up as proof, unwilling to let his gentle, competent fingers undo anything else.

He smiled and led her down the wooden steps. They felt warm beneath her bare feet, just like the sand and the sun—and Mateo's skin.

Trailing behind him in the fine, yielding sand, Beth sternly called herself to order. She was Beth. A widow, middle-aged, shelf-expired—she'd be a crazy cat lady if it weren't for her allergy. She was not Beth, the sensual being who slurped creamy carbonara and wondered how it would feel to touch her visitor...

"Oh," she groaned when she noticed what she was doing and slapped a hand to her forehead. Maybe she had a fever, or maybe the sun had fried her brain. She missed Ben every day, but not like this. Where was this sudden desire coming from?

Mateo bent to pick up a piece of sea glass. He walked to the water's edge and rinsed it off. "Beth, come here," he called, waiting until she stood by his side.

"What color of sea glass is your favorite?" he asked, holding out the glass in a closed fist so she couldn't see it.

"Blue," she said automatically, her thoughts still busy with the new feelings she was experiencing. "I always like blue best."

He chuckled, opening his hand. "Bad luck for me. It's only green."

Beth's eyes widened as she saw the glass. It was as big as a robin's egg. The rolling tides had sanded and tumbled and polished and buffed the glass, and the salt of eons had etched it with kisses until the green turned the ethereal color of fairy wings and angel eyes. "Wow," she breathed, taking the glass from his palm, barely noticing the brush of her fingers against his hand. "It's beautiful."

"Ah." He nodded, rubbing sand off his hand. "So, you like it after all?"

"I love it." She smiled up at him, delighted by the gift. "I never thought about it before. I just always look for blue out of habit."

"But you like the green?" He smiled as the breeze tousled his hair, clasping his hands behind his back.

"I love the green," she said, gazing again at the treasure. It was silly to adore a piece of sea glass, but it was happening. "Sometimes, you have to see it to fall in love, don't you?"

"Ah, yes," he agreed, nodding thoughtfully. "Sometimes, you do." He gently tipped her chin up with his finger, catching her gaze. "Beth?"

Startled, she blinked into his eyes. "What?"

"The house over there?" He pointed to a house further down the beach. "That's where I live." With his hands behind his back again, he smiled peculiarly at her. "I'm heading over. Can you find your way back?"

"Of course." It was a straight line of beach that connected their houses. "Of course I can. Thank you for the carbonara, Mateo, and the company."

"You are most welcome." Already, he was taking backward steps toward his house, his eyes still holding hers.

"And for..." She raised the sea glass with a smile. "I really love it."

"I'm glad." A flicker of something unreadable passed across his face before he smiled, waved, and turned, walking quickly toward his house.

"Bye," Beth whispered, tugging down her fluttering dress and brushing a curl from her eyes.

Was he running away? Had she said something wrong?

She clutched the sea glass in her hand, tracing their steps back to her cottage. Maybe it would be better if Mateo ran. A man like him—he wouldn't want to date an aging widow. Perhaps that's what he had realized when that peculiar look crossed his face.

The sea glass warmed in her palm, as warm as the sand, the sun, Mateo's skin.

"Beth, really," she whispered, scolding herself as she climbed the wooden steps back to her garden. "Do me a favor and stop, will you? Lusting after your neighbor isn't dignified."

But he brought me carbonara—the secret family recipe, no less, a bratty inner voice replied. Beth almost jumped; she hadn't heard that voice since her twenties. *And he picked you red roses and found you the most beautiful sea glass.*

"Enough," she muttered, sitting down to slip back into her wedge sandals. "Enough, enough, enough."

His touch made your heart flutter. And you're no longer married.

Determined to drown out that rebellious little voice, Beth pulled her phone from her pocket. She'd listen to an audiobook, something soothing to quiet her mind. But first, she saw she had missed a text.

Wondering when you were thinking of picking me up. It's okay if you changed your mind, just let me know.

Irritated with herself and feeling guilty for forgetting her responsibilities, Beth dialed the number. At least she had prepared the bedroom the night before, washing the linens, mopping the floors, and cleaning the upstairs bathroom with the wide porcelain tub. There was still more to do, but it was already cozy, clean, and livable.

When the line picked up, she cleared her throat, ensuring her voice sounded steady. "Lily, sweetheart, are you all packed? Yes, I'm coming right now. I'm sorry I'm calling so late—I got caught up in something here for a moment. See you in ten minutes."

CHAPTER 11

L ily sat in the front room of the hotel, watching the soft, colored lights from the sea-glass chandelier dance across the walls. The hotel was beautiful, but her heart ached to be back in Mendocino Beach. Her mother's body had arrived last night, and she'd just gotten the call from the funeral home confirming the service. It was really going to happen now.

She twisted her hands in her lap, anxiety bubbling up. Getting her mother's remains to this point had been a long, grueling process—so much paperwork, formalities, and red tape to fulfill Mom's final wish of being laid to rest in her hometown. Now, though, as the moment approached, Lily wasn't sure what to feel.

"Lily?"

She looked up to see Audrey Summers, the young hotel manager, standing in the doorway.

"Yes?"

"Beth is here." Audrey smiled. "Are you ready to meet her?"

"Sure." Lily rose and picked up her suitcase. "Thanks again for putting me up, Audrey."

"You're so welcome." Audrey tilted her head.

"Are you sure I can't pay for the room?"

"No worries. When my mom first got here, she was glad to have a place to stay. I'm just paying it forward. It's all good." She looked up. "Hey, if you end up staying in town a little longer, come hang out. My friends and I could always use more company. There aren't many young people around here, especially this time of year."

Lily managed a small smile. "I appreciate that."

"Really, don't hesitate. I'm starting to rent rooms to college students next semester, but until then, the place is pretty quiet." Audrey's grin widened. "We could use the reinforcements."

"Got it. Thanks again." Glancing out the window, Lily noticed that Beth was talking to someone in the parking lot. There was no rush. "Is your mom helping you run the hotel?" she asked, remembering the older woman who had been around.

Audrey laughed. "That's my great-aunt. My mom and her husband own a vineyard up in the hills. You should visit sometime—it's gorgeous. Picture golden hills, warm nights, and fireflies."

"Maybe," Lily said, though her heart wasn't in it. Not now, with the funeral looming. She wasn't in the mood to hang out or enjoy warm summer nights.

"Oh, looks like your ride is ready. Bye, Lily. Nice meeting you. Good luck with everything. Let me know if you need my help."

"Thank you," Lily said quietly as Beth waved her over. "Bye."

"Sorry I'm late." Beth thrust a thumb over her shoulder. "I just ran into an old friend."

"I'm just glad you came at all," Lily blurted out, surprising herself. The truth was, she did need someone right now—someone to help shoulder the weight she felt pressing down on her chest. Beth had offered to be one of the people Lily could lean on. And with all her grown-up twenty-eight years, Lily really, really wanted someone to lean on. Despite being skilled, independent, and capable, she suddenly felt like a child in need of comfort.

"Of course I came," Beth said, smiling as she led Lily to the car.

Lily blinked as they stepped out into the bright afternoon sun. It was beautiful. Even in her state, she could see that. "You know, if I weren't here to bury my mother, I'd love to explore the area." She lifted her suitcase into the backseat and slid into the passenger seat next to Beth. "Audrey just told me about a winery."

"It's gorgeous," Beth said as she started the car. "So are the beaches. There's also a lighthouse nearby, and the ferry ride to the island is beautiful—especially if you stroll along Wedding Lane."

"Wedding Lane?" Lily asked, glancing out the window at the passing scenery.

"All the shops you'd need for a wedding," Beth explained. "I got my dress there ages ago. Jenny, Audrey's mom, bought hers there too when she married the vintner. That was a stunning dress, by the way."

"Sounds fun." Lily was feeling better now that she was with Beth, on her way to Mendocino Beach and Grandma's house. Even though she barely knew Beth, it almost felt as if Lily had family in town. "Any other time, I'd go to have a look. But I had a call from the funeral home. My mother's body has arrived. I can go later this afternoon."

"I'm glad she's finally here," Beth said softly, glancing over at her. "Audrey mentioned you haven't eaten anything today. Are you hungry?"

"I'm hungry, but I don't have an appetite."

"Well, you have to eat something. Can I take you out?"

Lily turned to Beth, surprised by the offer. "You'd take me out?"

"Of course. You've been through enough, child. You need nourishment." Beth smiled, turning down a smaller road. In the distance, Lily could see the shimmering Pacific. "I also feel bad about the beach house. It should've gone to you."

Lily shrugged. "It's fine. I would've liked it, but it was Mom's to do with what she wanted. Maybe she owed your husband something. My mom had a lot of chaotic energy, you know? She sparkled with it."

"Sounds like she was lovely, but I'm not sure that's the explanation." Beth shook her head as she parked the car. "My husband wasn't one to lend money. I handled the finances—I would've known."

Lily opened her door. "I was just saying." They stood in front of a small restaurant called Le Pélican.

Beth came to stand beside her. "Lily?"

"Yes?"

"Why do you think your mother left the house to Ben? Do you think the two of them had an affair?"

Lily bit her lip. "Did you love your husband?"

Beth nodded. "Very much."

"Then...why don't we leave it? At least for now. It's not going to change anything." Lily hugged herself. "I'm barely hanging on. If I think about these things too much, I might... I don't know. Break down or something."

"Of course. I do apologize." Beth's questions had to wait. Lily was not responsible for her mother's behavior, nor was this the time to find out more about Margaret's past. Right then and there, Beth decided to put the girl first and let her bring up the topic herself—when she was ready to confide in Beth. "You do have enough to deal with," she said gently and pushed open the door. They stepped into the restaurant, the comforting aroma of freshly baked bread and simmering sauces wrapping around them like a hug.

A petite woman appeared in the doorway, her face beaming. "Welcome, ladies. I have just the perfect dishes for you today," she declared staunchly, leading them to a cozy corner table by the window. The table was elegantly set with a pristine white tablecloth, gleaming china, polished silverware, sparkling glasses, and a small vase of fresh lavender that added a gentle, soothing fragrance to the air.

"Her name is Marta," Beth whispered as they followed her. "She owns the restaurant, and she is an incredible cook."

Lily settled into her chair, glancing out the window to see the serene stretch of ocean in the distance. The calming view contrasted with her emotions, settling her nerves. "Don't feel bad about the house," she said, once Beth had stowed her purse. "Mom always did things her own way. I'm used to it by now." She offered a wistful smile.

Beth hesitated before speaking, a confession lingering in her tone. "I'm glad you're staying with me. No matter why Ben inherited the house, you'll always have a place to stay whenever you come to Mendocino Beach."

Lily was surprised by the offer. "Thank you. I might take you up on that." She paused, her voice softening. "But...aren't you angry with your husband?"

Beth sighed, her eyes drifting toward the shimmering ocean outside. "You know, he's gone," she said, sounding more matter-of-fact than her expression let on. "He's not here for me to get mad at him. I'd still like to know. It would make a difference to know for certain he was faithful to me. But there's nothing I can do about it either way."

Before Lily could respond, Marta arrived with a steaming tray of appetizers. "We need to get your appetite up," she said sternly, wagging a finger at Lily in a playful but firm manner. "You're wasting away."

"In her defense," Beth explained, "Lily's mother just passed."

"Ah no, ma poor chérie." Marta gave a quick, understanding nod before setting the tray down. "Scallops," she announced proudly before disappearing into the kitchen.

Lily blinked at the tray. Usually, she ordered what she liked from the menu. Apparently, not here. Here, the restaurant owner told you what you got.

"Well." Beth smiled at Lily. "In her defense, when it comes to food, she always knows best. Help yourself and enjoy. And don't worry about the bill. I have an account here."

"Oh. Thank you." It was a relief. Between her income and her inheritance, Lily was by no means penniless. Still, exclusive French restaurants were not in the budget she set herself.

The scallops were a vision, perfectly seared with a golden-brown crust that gleamed under the soft lighting. They were nestled on a bed of rich, buttery mashed potatoes, swimming in a fragrant white wine and shallot sauce. Garnished with fresh parsley and a touch of delicate black truffle, the dish looked irresistible.

Lily inhaled the intoxicating aroma, and although seafood wasn't usually her favorite, she suddenly craved it. Tentatively, she took a bite, combining a piece of scallop with a bit of the creamy mash.

"Mmm." The surprised sound escaped her as she covered her mouth, her eyes locking with Beth's, who watched with amusement.

"Good?" Beth asked, her smile widening.

The scallop melted in Lily's mouth before she could answer, its tender sweetness balanced perfectly by the savory richness of the sauce. The mashed potatoes were luxurious, smooth, and comforting—a perfect contrast.

"This is amazing," Lily whispered, her small smile growing. "I didn't know I liked scallops."

Beth leaned forward, encouraging. "Have more," she said. "Have them all."

Lily shook her head. "We'll share. I want you to enjoy them too."

"You do?" Beth's smile deepened, a touch of warmth lighting her eyes.

Lily shrugged, scooping more seafood and buttery potatoes onto both of their plates. "It's even better when you can share the experience."

Beth leaned back and picked up her fork. "You know," she said, popping a scallop in her mouth, "I'll enjoy having you stay at the cottage. I can't wait to have coffee with you in the garden. It's so pretty when the morning fogs lift, and everything smells of the sea and lavender and roses. It opens the heart and the soul and airs you out."

Chewing, Lily nodded. "I'm looking forward to it too, Beth. I feel like I need airing out."

"Ah oui, I knew you would like the appetizer." Marta had arrived with two steaming plates, which she slid in front of the women. "Duck à l'orange," she declared. "I started it this morning. I just knew someone would come for it." She threw Beth a sharp, disapproving glance. "You ate before you came here."

"I'm sorry." Beth looked so guilty that Lily almost chuckled. "It's over an hour ago."

"Don't do it again!" Marta said bossily before sailing back toward her kitchen, taking the empty scallop tray and appetizer plates.

"Wow," Beth said, following her path. "Close call." She chuckled, but Lily swallowed as the warm aromas of thyme and roast meat reached her. The duck, its skin perfectly caramelized with an orange glaze, was served alongside tender green beans and a fragrant herb-speckled rice pilaf.

"This looks fantastic," Lily whispered when Marta had disappeared from view. She was a little scared of the cook. "Did you really eat already?"

"No worries, I can eat again." Beth picked up her fork. "Besides, I always feel better when I'm here. Go ahead and try it. It really helps not to be starving on top of grieving."

"I think you're right. I do feel a bit better already." Lily could already feel the effect of the first course, her body waking up.

Maybe it was the food—the rich, savory dishes filling her with warmth and giving her body strength—or maybe it was the knowledge that she'd soon be staying at her beloved grandmother's house. Or perhaps it was Beth's steady, comforting presence. Whatever it was, everything suddenly felt just a little bit better. And as Lily ate every delicious bite of her dish, she realized that a little bit better was exactly what she needed to keep moving forward.

Chapter 12

Gently, Beth closed the door behind her and stepped onto the patio, inhaling a deep, slow breath.

Lily had gone to bed an hour ago, after returning from the funeral home. She'd taken a bath, using the salts and candles Beth had bought for her—small comforts for a difficult night.

Beth hadn't heard a peep from her room since, not even the sound of soft crying. The last soft gurgle of water in the pipes had long gone quiet by the time Beth had tiptoed upstairs to check that all the candles were extinguished. Lily had carried a vanilla-scented one into her bedroom.

When Beth returned downstairs, it was barely after eight. The sky was already preparing for dusk, casting the last of its golden light across the ocean. It was Beth's favorite time of day—the calm just before nightfall.

The air was cooler now, the heat of the day fading with the light. The sounds of the world softened as well, settling into an evening lull. Even the smell of the gardens changed as the roses and daisies closed their blossoms for the night, and the scents of sea and drying kelp emerged, dancing with the notes of beach heather, California laurel, and hummingbird sage to the coast's native symphony.

She picked up the shawl she'd slung over the chair on the patio and draped it around her shoulders in case there were mosquitoes. Every so often, a confused bug would wander onto the beach, carried by the breeze.

Picking a small bouquet of lavender and sage as she walked through the garden, Beth descended the stairs, left her sandals behind, and stepped onto the beach. The golden sand still radiated the heat of the sun, and tempted by the cool water, Beth lifted the hem of her dress and waded ankle-deep into the red-golden water, swirling the sand as she walked.

"Beth?"

Startled, she looked up. "Mateo!" Her heart skipped a beat as she saw him, dark eyes gleaming, his silver-black curls dancing in the breeze. He ran a hand through them, pushing them back. The sleeves of his linen shirt were rolled up, and the edges of his pants darkened from seawater. He must have been walking along the shore, just like her.

"I didn't mean to surprise you," Mateo said, stepping closer. "I'm just not used to seeing anyone else out here this late."

"You didn't." She smiled. "I was just lost in thought. How are you?"

"Good." He spread his hands. "Long day at the restaurant, but I'm glad to be home." His gaze softened. "You haven't come by in a while." He easily fell into step with her, walking on the sand while she stayed in the water.

"I've been cheating on you, I'm afraid," she said with a teasing smile, her heart fluttering as their eyes met. "I went to Le Pélican today."

"Hmm?" He looked down, meeting her eye.

"Le Pélican." Beth lowered her gaze to the water playing around her feet again. If she locked eyes with him too long, she would blush like a maiden. Already, her throat and jawline felt warm. "I have a guest who needed a pick-me-up, and Le Pélican seemed like the thing."

"There is no competing with Marta," Mateo said philosophically. "It would be foolish to try. The best I can do is keep her favor."

"You are an excellent chef," Beth said shyly. "And I truly love eating your food, Mateo. It makes me warm and happy inside."

The set of his shoulders softened as he put a hand to his heart. "That means a lot to me, Beth. Thank you."

"Um...no, thank you." Now Beth really was flushing warmly, and her blushing got even worse when she saw that Mateo noticed, the laugh lines near his eyes crinkling. Distracted, she stepped on a shell and stumbled before catching herself. "Oh, shoot," she murmured, gathering the dripping material of her long skirt.

"Take my arm, Beth." Mateo offered it. "You do not want to fall in the water. I tried it before and recommend staying warm and dry."

Beth eyed his arm. Again, the sleeves of his shirt were rolled up, and she remembered well the feelings that had overtaken her the last time she'd touched his bare skin. I'm all right, she braced to say. "Thank you," were the words that actually left her lips before she slipped her arm through his.

It was fine. She'd only rest her fingers with the slightest of touches on his arm. Just barely. She was old, she was wise, she could do it without reacting to his touch like a teenage girl.

Mateo immediately foiled that plan by placing his other hand on hers, naturally pressing it closer. "Are you comfortable?" he asked with his soft, warm voice.

Beth took a few steps before she stopped. Electric twinges sailed from his hand straight to her heart and her soul. She couldn't do this. He was too handsome, too nice, and the romantic sunset surrounding them did nothing to keep her grounded. "My dress is wet," she murmured. "I think I should go back."

"Ah." He nodded and let her go. "But going back, you will be uncomfortable with the wet linen wrapping around your legs." His gaze wandered from her eyes to her legs. "Let's sit and rest and let it dry before you leave, no?"

"Okay." Beth was starting to feel weak in the knees. If he looked at her again like that, she might faint. Maybe it was a good idea to sit down for a moment.

"I have..." He turned to look at the beach, assessing exactly where they were. "I have a blanket." Smiling at her to follow, he led the way up the beach to a nook in the seagrass, where Beth spotted a cream-colored blanket and a backpack. Nearby was a small ring of stones containing a small stack of driftwood.

"Here. Rest, Bella. Your skirt will dry in no time, and then you can walk back." Mateo offered her his hand for support.

Beth took it and sat down. "This is nice," she said, realizing with a hitch in her breathing that this was even more romantic than walking along the water. It was hard to stay composed in the face of such simple romance—the two of them alone on the beach, under the glow of the moon.

"I often come down here to cook my dinner," Mateo explained and sat beside her, pulling over the backpack. "After working all day in the kitchen, I like a change."

"Do you get tired of cooking?"

The light in his eyes twinkled as he pulled out matches and lit one, holding it to the dry kelp below the stacked driftwood. "Never tired of cooking," he said. "But of being inside, yes. So when I come home, I swap the stove for the fire. It awakens something primordial in me." He glanced at her, waggling his eyebrows like a villain.

"I'd probably just have leftovers," Beth said, watching flames lick up the bleached branches.

"No. No. Bella, not leftovers." He shook his head. "I will cook your food if all you have is leftovers."

A brief vision of Mateo, cooking dinner in her kitchen, flitted through Beth's mind. "Oh," she said weakly. "Yeah, I don't mind leftovers. Some dishes are better the next day."

"Ah." He nodded, trying to be understanding, but the nod soon morphed into shaking his head. "Who takes care of you that you eat leftovers, Beth? Nobody?"

"I take care of me." She cleared her throat. "What about yourself? Um. Do you have someone...like...a girlfriend?" It felt like being fifteen again. Only the kids nowadays were probably a lot cooler than she was.

He turned to look at her over his shoulder, grinning. "I have no girlfriend, no wife, no boyfriend, nothing. I spend my days perfecting my spaghetti carbonara, crying at night because I am lonely." The light of the flames danced over his jaw, skipping across the clean line of his nose, catching the laughter in his eyes.

Beth had to grin back. She might be old, but she was no fool. The man was too impossibly handsome to cry alone at night. "I'm sure you have company every now and then."

Mateo chuckled, shrugging a confession. "Maybe," he admitted unabashedly. "Every now and then. But they always run from me."

Beth lowered herself to her elbows. The fine sand shifted under her blanket, cradling her comfortably. "Why do they run?" Asking for a friend...

Mateo pulled a merino sweater from the backpack, balled it up, and offered it as a pillow. "Some don't want a cook. Others only visit the California coast." He winked at Beth. "Other times again, it is me who runs."

"Why do you run, then?"

"That too—it differs."

"Give me examples." She rested her head on his sweater. The soft wool smelled like him, warm and inviting, with lingering, smoky notes of thyme and olives that evoked feelings of home, warmth, and nurturing.

"Why do you want examples?" Meeting her eyes, he smiled while pulling a folded barbeque rack from the pack and arranging it over the flames. "What good is it to know?"

"I've not dated much," Beth admitted. "I pretty much met Ben and married him. It's the sum total of my romantic past."

"Your husband, Ben," Mateo murmured. "He must have been a good man."

"He was." Beth nodded, stirring up Mateo's scent. "So tell me. Why do you run?"

CHAPTER 13

Mateo pulled a plastic bag from his pack, unwrapping two seasoned steaks that he placed on the makeshift grill. "The last lady, I liked her. But she didn't eat. No carbs, no cheese, no bread." His eyebrows rose in exasperation. "How can I be with her?"

Beth giggled. "I can see how that is a problem. What else?"

"One didn't like the beach."

Beth pulled her chin back. "Who doesn't like the beach?"

He lifted his hands in a helpless gesture. "I don't know! I don't know. The sand bothered her. She didn't care for shells or sea glass or sand dollars. Even if they were immaculate." He glanced at her.

She smiled. "Are those your criteria for picking a partner? Must like carbs and the beach?"

Chuckling, he flipped the steaks. "Am I wrong? Are those not good criteria?"

Beth had to laugh too, not bothering to answer. She could tell he wasn't telling her everything. After all, they were just getting to know each other.

A gull screamed and swooped low; Mateo was busy cooking and opening a bottle of red wine, and Beth relaxed into the beauty of the falling night. The sun had sunk into the sea, leaving a velvety blue night and a rising moon of gold and silver to care for the earth.

"I only brought one glass," Mateo said and lowered himself onto the blanket beside Beth. Only glowing embers were left of the fire, radiating warmth and the delicious smell of the seasoned steaks into the cooling air. Beth watched as he filled the glass with ruby-red wine and handed it to her.

"Let's share," she said, smiling as she accepted it. She sipped, savoring the deep, woody notes. Mateo propped up his elbow and rested his head on his hand. "The real reason I've never married is that none of them were the one," he said after a moment. "So I find something I don't like. A little thing that makes it easy to let go."

She handed him the glass and laid back down on her soft pillow. "Unless it's love at first sight, you'll risk missing her. Don't you think so?"

He lowered the glass. "How was it for you and Ben?"

She turned to him. "We had rough patches," she admitted. "It's not always easy going when you're married."

He sighed. "I'm not a complicated person. I like it when love is easy. I don't enjoy drama, fights, angst."

She smiled again. "Does anyone?"

"Yes." He lifted an eyebrow. "Yes, there are people who enjoy it."

"So what do you do when there is conflict?"

"Talk." He set the glass down and sat up, circling his arms around his knees. "I know my feelings, and I go to the trouble of explaining them. I listen, too."

"I see." Beth hesitated, choosing her words carefully. "So let's say things are going well, but then...the woman expresses a feeling you might not respect."

"Like what?"

"Like..." She swallowed, her voice dropping. "Desire. What if she feels...desire?"

"For me?" He smiled at her. "As long as it's me she desires, I respect it very much. I'm not sure I understand. What do you mean?"

Her chest tightened at his words. His openness felt unfamiliar, disarming. "Oh. Nothing, really." Embarrassed, Beth wished she'd kept her mouth shut. In her marriage, desire had often led to a quiet, uncomfortable space. Ben had never really spoken about it, leaving her to wonder how he truly felt. She'd sensed, more often than not, that her desire had been...unwelcome.

But Ben had been a good man—kind, gentle, always loving her in his own way. He was steady, a wonderful provider, someone she could trust with anything. Yet, he lived in his head more than in his body. Physical closeness, the rawness of passion, had never been where their connection thrived. She'd learned to quiet that part of herself, to push it aside, thinking it was just how things were supposed to be.

"How long were you married?" Mateo asked softly after a short, awkward pause. "To the one man you have known."

"Um. Decades." She didn't care to tell him how many.

"Ah." He nodded slowly. "And you were married so young. It is how it should be, but maybe, neither one of you knew what to do for the other."

Her eyes widened at the direction of the conversation. "You mean...like that?"

"Yes." He refilled the glass and handed it to her. "It takes practice."

"Oh, heaven," Beth whispered and took the glass, drinking deeply, trying hard not to think about her and Ben's first nights together. Of course it had gotten better over time. Of course it'd been good. They'd found their rhythm, settled into what was comfortable, but...she'd wondered. Was that all there was?

"Heaven is where it should take you." She heard the laughter in Mateo's voice but refused to look at him. "Ah, Bella." He took the empty glass from her hand. "Let's talk about your Ben. I want to know what made him so special to you."

Beth took a deep breath. "He had a way of making every day feel like an adventure. He adored me, and he always surprised me with gifts and acts of love. He took good care of me, and I really loved him."

"He sounds like a good man," Mateo said. The last light of the embers played on his face as he rose to stoke them, adding another log. "Ben lit your way."

"He lit my way," Beth agreed, thinking how apt the words were. Ben truly had illuminated her path.

Mateo nodded. "Tell me more about him."

While he put the steaks on paper plates and added sides from containers in his pack, Beth talked. Haltingly at first, but soon more fluid. They ate and drank the wine, and her words streamed, lightening the weight of missing Ben as if Mateo was not only sharing his wine but her grief, lifting the burden weighing down her heart. Finally, the flow of words ebbed to a trickle, and Beth lowered her empty plate. "I'm sorry, Mateo," she said, suddenly embarrassed. "I don't usually talk about myself so much."

"Don't be." He smiled, taking the plates and tossing them into the fire. They watched as the flames licked at the paper. "I'm glad you did. I'm glad to know you better."

The night, with its gentle sea breeze and moonlit sky, felt intoxicating. Beth's head swam with a mix of wine, memories, and the unexpected warmth of Mateo's company. She glanced at him, her voice soft when she spoke. "It's been wonderful. All of this. Thank you, Mateo."

"You want to go home?" His eyes lingered on hers.

"Yes." She nodded. "I should probably head back."

"The beach house or the house you and Ben built?"

Without hesitation, she answered, "The beach house. I really shouldn't drive anymore." She lifted the empty wine glass, giving him a sheepish smile.

"I'll drive you," he said, taking the glass and packing it away. "If that's where you want to go, Beth."

"Oh. Thank you, but that's okay." She didn't even have to think about the offer. After everything they'd shared that evening, she didn't want to be alone in the vast house she once shared with Ben. She wanted the comfort of the cozy beach cottage—the small room with its sea views, where the moon would rise and the tide would hum her to sleep. She wanted to wake up and drink coffee with Lily in the garden, walk along the shore to feel the cold ocean nip at her ankles, and search for sea glass.

"That's okay," she repeated, softer this time, reaching out. Her fingertip traced the hard, stubbled line of Mateo's jaw, something she'd longed to do all evening.

Mateo gently caught her hand, curling her fingers into his and pressing a light kiss on her knuckles. "I'll walk you back," he said quietly. "Now that your dress is dry, I don't want you stumbling into the water again."

He rose, offering his hand to her, slipping her arm beneath his just as he'd done before. They walked across the silver-tinged sand, back to the stairs leading up to her garden.

Beth wanted to ask if he'd like to come in for coffee, the thought lingering on her lips. But before she could decide, Mateo inclined his head in that familiar, gentlemanly way, waved good night, and disappeared into the night.

Her mind swirling with thoughts, wine, and new feelings, Beth hurried along her rambling, sleeping garden into the cottage. Once inside, she went upstairs and locked herself into the room with the four-poster bed. She took a long, hot bath before curling into the freshly washed bed sheets. Miraculously, she felt herself quickly drifting into sleep. The last thing she heard was the rushing of the sea, the last thing her drowsy gaze met a golden moon rising peacefully into the night sky.

CHAPTER 14

B eth stood in the middle of the old bookstore, the cozy, familiar scent of aged paper and bound volumes enveloping her. She and Hannah had set up a circle of plush armchairs around a small wooden table and draped each seat with a soft, knitted throw. The table was laden with a selection of pastries, cheese, and a steaming pot of herbal tea. Flickering candles cast a warm glow, creating an inviting atmosphere as night settled over the rushing waves of the Pacific, perfect for their book club meeting.

Hannah arrived, mismatched mugs from the back of the store in her hands. They both looked up when the small gold bell over the store door tinkled, and Sara walked in, her face lighting up as she entered the welcoming space.

"Hannah, Beth, this is perfect!" Sara exclaimed, hugging her friends tightly. "I've been so looking forward to our book club."

Hannah laughed and dropped into one of the soft, deep chairs, kicking off her loafers and pulling her legs up. "Me too. Have you read all the chapters?"

"Almost. Not quite," Sara admitted, settling into another of the armchairs and wrapping a throw around her shoulders. "It was a busy week."

"Same here." Beth poured tea and handed out steaming mugs before sinking into the last chair. "Poor Lily. I wish I could help her more."

"You're doing everything you can," Hannah reassured her. "How is she doing?"

"The funeral is tomorrow," Beth murmured. "It's so hard. I wish I could do more for her."

"I'm sure you do," Hannah said loyally. "You keep her company. Sometimes, that's the only thing you can do."

"Are you going to the funeral with Lily?" Sara asked, taking a sip of her tea. "Or is it complicated because of the connection to Ben?"

"Lily asked me to come," Beth said, feeling her forehead crinkle at the reminder. "And since I inherited the house, I already feel a sense of obligation to my unknown benefactress."

"It's the right thing to do. And it will help Lily to have you there," Hannah agreed. "Let us know if you want company to decompress afterward. We're here for you."

Beth nodded. "There is something so unsettling about a delayed funeral. You are floating in limbo between having and losing. It's a very difficult space to occupy."

"Talking about difficult spaces to occupy," Sara said and picked a cube of Gouda cheese. "You have a rosy glow about you, Hannah."

"Glow?" Beth looked up, puzzled. "Oh, you do! Look at you! All rosy-cheeked."

"Beard stubble, I reckon." Sara smiled. "Let me guess. Alex is back?"

"Yes." Grinning, Hannah rubbed her rosy cheek. "He is. Why? What difficult space are you referring to?"

"Is he staying? Or is he leaving again?" Sara shrugged.

Hannah's gaze dropped. "I don't know."

Sara tapped a finger to her chin. "So he might leave anytime?"

"Maybe." Hannah avoided her friends' eyes. "Maybe not."

"Alex claims you're the long-lost love of his life, and all he has for you is a maybe, maybe not?" Sara exchanged a glance with Beth and set down her cup.

"It's fine," Hannah said. "How is the Gouda? Is it good? I asked for the good one."

But Sara was not to be distracted, stapling her fingers. "Let me see, let me see."

"No," Hannah said weakly and pulled her knees closer to her chest, protecting herself from what was to come.

Sara grinned. "A mysterious ex-military man who returns suddenly, and a girlfriend who's tight-lipped about him... Hmm."

Beth turned her gaze between her friends, absorbing Sara's implications. "So, am I right in assuming you can neither confirm nor deny what's going on?" Sara asked.

Hannah sighed and then chuckled. "I can neither confirm nor deny whatever it is you think. But Alex would probably prefer we keep any speculation to ourselves. And if we must speculate, let's stick to doing it in this bookstore. Promise?"

"Ooh, what, do we think there are spy bugs hidden in the bakery?" Sara giggled.

"Sara," Beth chided lightly. "Come on, that's none of our business. I don't want to think about spies every time I buy a loaf of sourdough."

"Bookstore only," Hannah repeated calmly.

"Fine. Pinkie promise," Sara agreed. She turned to Beth. "Beth? This store only. Got it?"

Beth laughed. "I promise. Pinkie promise. Girl Scout promise. Spit-twice-and-die promise." She held up her hands. "I don't want trouble with...anyone."

"Exactly," Hannah said, satisfied. She drained her tea and opened her book. "So, let's get back to business. Where were we? Oh yes. This book is quite scandalous, isn't it?"

"Absolute smut," Sara confirmed happily. "I don't know how they come up with this stuff. None of this ever even occurred to me, and I'm in my forties." She thought for a moment. "Nor, I regret to say, has any of it occurred to Andy. Where do they find these men?"

"In the highlands," Hannah suggested. "It must be the bracing mountain air."

"It's that breakfast porridge," Beth guessed, laughing. "All that fiber is good for vascular health."

"I tried it, but I just can't get used to porridge. What did they put on their oatmeal?" Sara asked. "Wild blueberries? They are only in season for, like, two weeks."

"I don't know. And I don't care. I don't want to think about the hero eating porridge with blueberries when he has all these other redeeming qualities," Hannah declared and knocked on the wooden table to call the ladies to order. "Now. What do you think about her sister telling on the tryst she discovered?"

"Goodness, not much," Sara said heartlessly. "Where's her sense of sisterhood? What a little tattle-tale."

Beth chuckled. "It's more complex than that. She faced a moral dilemma."

They continued on about their latest read, a historical romance that had everyone alternatingly blushing and swooning. But despite the thrilling passages and interesting historical facts, despite the fluttering dresses and drawn swords, Beth's mind was elsewhere. Finally, she couldn't hold it in any longer.

"Girls, stop for a moment. I have something to tell you," Beth interrupted a rambling speculation about the availability of coffee—caffe latte in particular—in the Scottish Highlands. Her voice wavered slightly.

Startled, Hannah and Sara turned their attention to her, concern and curiosity in their eyes.

"What is it?" Sara asked. "Are you okay? It's not about Maggie and Ben, is it?"

"Yes—no. I mean, no, since I don't know what happened between them, if anything. But I've decided to sell the house Ben built," she said, taking a deep breath. "And I'm moving into the seaside cottage. No matter what may or may not have happened there in the past."

There was a moment of silence. Then, Hannah reached out and squeezed Beth's hand. "Good for you. But that's a big step. How does it make you feel?"

Beth sighed, looking down at her hands. "It's just... I need a fresh start. The cottage feels like a place where I can breathe again. I want a second chance at a life."

Sara leaned forward. "I'm glad you're doing this. Moving doesn't mean you're being disloyal to Ben."

"We'll be with you every step of the way," Hannah promised. "Let us know what you need."

Beth felt a weight lift off her shoulders at their words. She didn't need their approval, but it sure was nice to have. And they were right. Moving into the seaside cottage meant embracing her future.

"Selling is going to be a lot of work," she said, accepting a marzipan éclair from Sara. "But the house will deteriorate further without Ben maintaining it. It's too much house for just me." She bit into the éclair, letting it melt on her tongue. "If I had kids who were coming home to visit, maybe. But I don't. It's just me."

"Just wait," Hannah said, smiling. "The cottage will keep you plenty busy, especially if you want to do more renovations."

"And what about that new neighbor?" Sara's eyes sparkled with interest. "He's very attentive, don't you think? And so handsome..."

"He certainly is." Beth considered telling them about the night on the blanket on the beach, about the kiss he'd pressed on her hand, but then decided it was too soon. The night was hers and Mateo's for now. She'd keep it that way until she figured out what she wanted.

"What's the next step for selling the house?" Hannah asked, pouring more tea and helping herself to a raspberry scone.

"I should have our real estate agent over," Beth said, the reality of it sinking in. "He'll let me know what needs to be done before listing it."

"Only list when you're ready," Sara warned. "Julian knows some people from San Francisco who are looking for a big, private home. They'll snap it up for whatever price you ask."

"I wonder how it feels when money isn't a concern," Hannah mused. "I still want to have that fundraiser for the bookstore. Alex said he doesn't want to draw attention to the store, but I said it would draw more attention not to have a fundraiser. Everyone knows businesses need more than a handful of secondhand book sales to thrive."

"Let us know when you have a plan," Sara said. "And I'll make sure Julian's friends come by with their checkbooks."

Beth looked at her friend. "You talk a lot about your Julian," she noted playfully.

Sara arched her eyebrows. "He's not my Julian."

"Oh." Beth and Hannah exchanged smiles. Sara had previously lit up when talking about her boss, Mr. Sterling. But something had happened. Now, he was simply Julian.

"Let it go, girls," Sara said, her eyebrows dropping. "Nothing to see here."

"How is Andy?" Hannah asked, a note of concern in her voice. They both knew Andy wasn't treating Sara as well as she deserved. Sara often looked tired, and she handled most of the household and childcare responsibilities on top of being the family breadwinner. Andy helped but only minimally, requiring constant reminders and lists.

Beth sighed. Maybe Andy was one of those people Mateo had mentioned, seeking drama rather than sharing responsibilities.

"Do you want to text your real estate agent now?" Hannah asked, maybe noticing Beth's distraction.

"Now?"

"While we're here for support," Hannah said.

"Okay." Beth's heart raced, but the morning in the cottage had convinced her to take the leap. The bright, sunny, cheerful room, the ocean singing outside, and the sweet scent of flowers in the air made up her mind. "Yes, actually, that would be nice." She pulled out her phone and found the real estate agent.

"What do I write?" she asked, her thumb hovering over the keys.

"Say you wonder whether he has time to stop by the house," Sara said without hesitation. "You're thinking about selling and want to talk, see if he's interested."

"Oh, he'll be interested," Hannah predicted confidently. "Ben's houses sell like hot crab cakes."

Her stomach squirming, Beth tapped the text. When she was done, she took a deep breath and locked eyes with her friends. "Right. Here goes." She hit send, and the text disappeared into the ether to find its recipient.

Beth set down the phone and glanced around the cozy bookstore. Slowly, a mix of nostalgia for the old times and hope for what was to come rose in her chest.

"How do you feel?" Hannah wanted to know.

"I feel...good." Beth paused, checking in with herself. "I feel good. I feel good!" She smiled, delighted to find that she was no longer scared. This felt right. Like a shifting train track that locked into a new position, sending her into brighter regions.

Hannah raised her teacup in a toast. "To new beginnings and the beautiful memories we'll always cherish."

Sara and Beth also raised their cups, clinking them together. "To new beginnings," they echoed.

Sipping her tea, a sense of tentative joy settled over Beth like a warm hug. The decision to move forward hadn't been easy. But with friends like Hannah and Sara at her side, she had the strength to face whatever came next. There was still so much promise of happiness in her future.

CHAPTER 15

The funeral for Lily's mother took place on a sunny afternoon in the little white church of Mendocino Beach. The salty breeze curled its way inside through the open door, bringing with it the fragrance of glittering waves and swaying lilac. The playful lightness of the day softened the heaviness in the air, easing some of the sorrow.

As small as it was, the church had been almost empty when Beth arrived. At first, it had been just Lily and her, sitting quietly in the front pew. Once Beth realized that Maggie had no other close family or friends in town, she quickly texted Hannah and Sara. The women had dropped everything they were doing and rushed to drum up support in the community, gathering as many as they could on short notice.

It was only a small crowd that gathered to pay their respects to the unknown mother and support the grieving daughter. At least Lily wasn't alone. And that, Beth thought, was what mattered most.

Beth smoothed her black skirt over her knees and looked up. The soft light filtering through the stained-glass windows cast hues of blue, green, and red onto the pews. A wreath of lilies and roses—Maggie's favorite flowers—stood near the coffin, filling the air with their fragrance.

As the last notes of the hymn faded, a quiet hush settled over the congregation. The pastor stepped forward, offering his final words, speaking of Margaret's spirit—her kindness, her laughter, and the love she'd given so freely.

Beth squeezed Lily's hand and fought to suppress her worry about how freely Maggie had truly loved. Instead, she focused on the pastor's words about strength and resilience, knowing they were shaped by Lily's own memories. After all, Lily had provided the notes for the eulogy; the pastor, who was new to town, had never known Maggie.

Then Lily stood and walked past the coffin, her fingers brushing the polished wood, eyes brimming with tears. She took a deep breath and began to speak, her voice trembling.

"My mother was unconventional," she began softly. "She never changed who she was to fit in. In fact, she never really did fit in. She felt it, deeply, I believe, but she accepted it." Lily paused, swallowing. "Like all people who don't change for others, she wasn't always easy to be with. But it also meant she was constant. And because of that, my mother was my anchor, however far apart we were. She was my guiding star." Her low voice carried the depth of her grief and her love.

Beth blinked back tears, her heart aching for Lily.

Not so long ago, Beth had walked down the same path. She'd lived too isolated, outside of town, building her life around Ben. After Ben was gone, there had been nothing left but an empty shell. If it weren't for that chance meeting with Hannah on the seawall one day...

Looking at the coffin, she wished Maggie could have had the luck of sitting down beside the right woman. Maybe she'd have found her community then.

Lily's voice pulled Beth back from her thoughts. "It's hard to sum a mother up in a few sentences, but I'll try. My mother was a brave woman. She embraced life. She wasn't afraid of showing her heart, though she sometimes hid her feelings. She saw beauty in the smallest things. She was fiercely independent, and she always tried her best to live life on her own terms. She was a traveler, and I inherited that from her. I think it's the reason we didn't have enough time together. I'll always regret not trying harder to make that happen." She had to clear her throat before she could carry on. "I truly believe that her love is still with me. And I hope it will guide me through whatever comes next. Because I miss her so much that I—I don't know. But I really need her."

Clearly miserable, Lily paused, looking out at the faces. Most of them strangers, but strangers who shared, or knew they would share, the loss she was suffering. Suddenly, a small smile tugged at the corner of Lily's mouth, even if her eyes shimmered with tears.

"Thank you all for being here, for coming to honor my mother. I didn't expect it. But it means the world to me."

She nodded that she had finished, placed a single white rose on the coffin, and went back to her seat.

Beth turned when she heard steps in the aisle. "Oh," she whispered, glancing at Hannah and Sara. "The pallbearers." The congregation rose in respectful silence as four men—fishermen from the village who helped the pastor when there was no family—came to carry the coffin to the cemetery.

Outside, the sky stretched bright and blue, and the warmth of the sun wrapped around them like a gentle hug. They followed the coffin to the gravesite. A playful breeze rustled through the eucalyptus trees, the sweet song of a bluebird drifted in the fragrant wind, and Beth hoped the loveliness of the day would soothe Lily during what would always be the hardest part of a funeral.

After the final prayer and the lowering of the coffin, the small crowd slowly dispersed, murmuring quiet words of comfort to Lily. Beth stayed by her side until everyone else had left.

"Ready to go home?" she asked softly, resting her hand on Lily's arm.

Lily nodded. Her eyes were red, but a small, grateful smile formed on her lips when she looked over. "I think so."

They walked together to Beth's car, the weight of the day heavy on their shoulders but softened by the peacefulness of closure. They drove away, the white church and cemetery fading in the rearview mirror.

As Beth and Lily pulled into the gravel driveway of the little seaside cottage, the familiar sound of the waves crashing against the shore greeted them. The sun had sunk lower in the sky, and a warm breeze stirred the lavender blooms that swayed along the path. The whitewashed walls of Maggie's cottage, weathered by the past, the salty air, and the wind, gleamed in the afternoon light.

Beth glanced over at Lily. The entire drive, she'd sat silently in the passenger seat, gazing out the window. Beth reached over and gave her hand a reassuring squeeze. "Hey. We're home," she said softly.

Lily blinked. "Tell me, Beth," she murmured, turning to her. "I thought the funeral was the hard part. Like a whirlwind of formalities and ceremony and duty. But now that it's over..." She rubbed her face with both hands. "I'm starting to think that there's nothing left to distract me from the loss."

"There's life," Beth said gently. "Life goes on." But she knew from experience that now came the quiet, where grief could settle in like a heavy weight. She swallowed a sigh, trying not to think of all the time and all the joy grief had already cost her.

They climbed out of the car, and Lily paused for a moment, staring at the cottage as if seeing it for the first time. To Lily, Beth realized, her mother's presence lingered in this place—in memories of the same weathered shutters, the rambling garden, the soft curtains fluttering in the open windows.

"Come on, sweetheart," she said, slipping Lily's arm under her own. "Let's go inside."

CHAPTER 16

A lex rubbed the water off his face, flicking icy drops at Hannah. She squealed and held up her beach towel to protect herself. "No! Hey! My notes!" She laughed, dabbing a drop off the paper.

"What's this?" He rolled on his back on the beach blanket beside her, squinting against the bright sun at the lines she'd scribbled.

She smiled at him. He looked terribly handsome in his black swim trunks, muscular and lean, with sea-water shimmering on his tan skin. "I'm organizing the benefit event for your bookstore."

"You don't have to do that," Alex said. "I promise I'll be all right. Let's just enjoy our time together." He rolled onto his side to see her better, gently tugging the notebook from her hands.

She curled her arms around her knees, trying not to laugh. They'd already talked about this, and she'd stood firm about making the little store pay for itself. No matter what the CIA paid their secret agents.

"What?" He grinned back, his eyes taking in her breezy teal cover-up—or rather, Hannah thought, the still-trim figure it veiled.

"How was the water?" she asked diplomatically.

"Cold. You look amazing."

"Hardly. I'm a middle-aged woman," she replied primly, tugging her cover-up close over her chest.

"And last time I looked, I'm a middle-aged man," he said in a low, seductive voice that sent goose-bumps down her spine, just as if he'd trailed his hand slowly down her warm, sensitive skin. "Talking about that...how about I bring you back home and you ask me in for a cup of tea?"

When they'd first started to date, Hannah had still felt insecure about the way she looked. But Alex had taught her that to him, her body was perfection.

She regarded him for a moment before she reached out, slowly running a finger along the hard line of his jaw. "Where is home?" she asked softly. "My place? Or your apartment over the bookstore?"

Catching her hand in his, he kissed her palm. His own hand was cold from swimming in the frigid water, but his lips were warm. "Home is where you are."

"Be serious," she said, lying down beside him, resting her head on her arm so she could look into his starry blue eyes. "Where is your home, Alex?"

It took him a while to answer. "I am serious, Hannah." He shrugged. "Before you came, it was the bookstore. But now Allison is staying there with Tommy."

"That's a temporary arrangement," Hannah replied, searching his face for clues that not having his own place was starting to wear on him. "You don't have to be homeless so you can help everyone around you,

you know? Giving the shirt off your back is one thing. Giving away your home is another."

He smiled. "Where is Allison supposed to go if I throw her out?"

"She'll always have a home with me." Hannah smiled back. "You know she does. And so does she."

Raising an eyebrow, he frowned. "You'd rather have her and Tommy stay with you than me?"

"If I thought it'd be a good idea, I'd ask you to move in for good today. But..." She tilted her head in question. "I'm not sure it is, Alex."

"Oh?" He sat up, shaking the sand off his gray T-shirt and pulling it over his head before glancing at her. "Have I overstayed my welcome?"

"No." She put a hand on his arm. "No, of course not. I love having you stay with me. But I suppose we should talk about it. Because..."

"Because—what, Hannah?" His voice was gentle. "Tell me."

"I just don't want to rush this," she said softly.

"Are we rushing?"

She thought about the whirlwind of love and sensuality and romance that had filled the days since his return from his secret mission. If it was up to her, she'd spend every single minute in his arms, by his side, in his bed.

But this was real life, not a fairytale. She and Alex were in their puppy love stage, and greedily, she was using it up all at once. After a long, cold marriage, Hannah knew she was overcompensating and taking too much now. She craved the intimacy, the connection, the warmth, the ease Alex brought to her life.

If she wasn't more careful, it would end soon.

Taking a deep breath, Hannah nodded. "Maybe we should slow down."

"Slow down," he repeated, his features turning to stone. "I don't want to slow down, Hannah. I thought we had a good time."

"We do. We have a great time. That's..." Embarrassed, she chuckled. "That's just it, Alex. I want it to last. I don't want you to get fed up with me. And I worry that if we're always together, you never get time to recover from me. Recharge the batteries, you know?"

His brow dropped, breaking the mask. "What are you talking about?"

"You know—suddenly you'll realize you need your own space and all that."

Running a hand through his wet hair, he said, "I don't—is that what happened with Evan?"

Hannah blew out a breath. She didn't want to bring Evan into their relationship. She didn't want to talk about the shame, the loneliness, the fear of abandonment he had trained her to expect. "You're mad."

"No, no." He dropped his hand. "I'm not mad. I'm trying to understand where this is coming from."

She bit her lips, cursing herself for having been so clumsy. She'd hurt his feelings. "I'm sorry, Alex. Everything is great. I'm so happy."

He shook his head. "Don't be sorry." He looked around for a towel, drying his face before talking. "I should be the one saying sorry. I've stayed at your house since I got back, and I never even asked if that's what you wanted. I'll better go grab my things."

Hannah stared at him in horror. What had happened? A moment ago, she'd been so happy and joyful, and now, she'd angered the man who had been there for her when she'd had nothing. "I didn't mean to... I love having you stay with me."

But it was too late. "Maybe you're right, Hannah." Alex sighed. "I'll talk with Allison as soon as she returns from visiting her mother, okay? She offered to move out before she left for San Francisco."

"No...that's not what I meant," Hannah said weakly. "I just thought we could talk."

"I'm glad we did." For a long moment, he studied her face. "You are right. I moved too fast. I assumed too much. I've loved you all my life, Hannah. But you just got divorced and need time to yourself. I see that now." He pulled his khaki pants over his dried swim trunks and picked up his towel, stuffing it into his backpack.

"Where are you going, Alex?" Despite the hot August sun, Hannah felt cold.

"It's almost time to open the store. I should get back there anyway." He smiled weakly. "Someone might want to buy a book this fine afternoon. You never know. And I should stop by the market to buy things."

"What about tonight?" she whispered. Since he'd returned, they'd spent all their time together. "Are you still going to come over?"

"I should clean the apartment. As much as I enjoy the scent of baby powder, I prefer not to sleep in it." He nodded at her. "What are you going to do?"

Hannah bit her lip. She'd planned on spending the night in his arms. "I suppose I also have some house cleaning to do. Do I see you tomorrow?"

"Maybe," he said gently. "I'll call you, okay? Bye, Hannah."

"Alex—"

He turned and ran a trembling hand through his hair. "I didn't expect this. But you're right. I really think I should go. I'll see you soon." He walked away, not looking back.

She drew a breath; this had gone badly. She'd hurt his feelings. And what if he was called back to service suddenly? She couldn't bear it if he'd suddenly left Mendocino Beach like this. "Bye, Alex," she said softly into the warm summer day. "I love you so much." But he was already too far away to hear.

CHAPTER 17

Cooper, the real estate agent who had handled most of Ben's home sales, tucked his clipboard under his arm. "It's good you decided to move," he said to Beth. "The house is a lot to handle. I can see the first signs of deterioration, and it would only get worse without regular maintenance." He turned to her. "No offense."

"None taken." Beth cleared her throat. "So you're going to list it soon?"

"I already have buyers I think would be excited to own this place. We don't have to list unless you want to." He winked. "But they'll pay whatever we ask. They've done it before."

Standing behind Cooper, Sara looked up with a satisfied expression. "I told you, Beth. People will snap up this gem before it hits the market."

"Really? Who are they?" Beth turned to look at Cooper. She didn't know him very well—Ben had been the one doing business with him.

"A large, lovely family, bursting at the seams with money," he said, busy straightening the note on his clipboard. "You'll have no problem. Unless you aren't quite ready to sell after all?" He shot her a glance. "It's okay. It's a beautiful house, and I understand that it's hard to let go. But you should let me know."

Beth closed her eyes and conjured up the image of her cozy cottage, her lovely garden, the shimmering sea beyond. "I made up my mind," she declared. "I'm ready to sell. Go ahead and give them a call."

"Fabulous!" Beaming, Cooper pulled out his cell phone. "I'll be just a moment," he said and stepped out onto the patio, pulling the door closed behind him.

"Are you okay?" Sara came to Beth, taking her hands. "You don't have to go forward if you're not ready. Take another couple of weeks."

"It's never going to be easy to move out," Beth said. "But I'm happier in the cottage. I might as well get it over with."

"Hire someone to do the packing," Sara recommended. "It's going to make things easier, especially since you're also renovating the cottage."

"That's a good idea. I will. There'll still be plenty left to organize and decide without me handling every little reminder of the last decade. I can't pack a book without reading a few pages, you know?"

"I do know." Sara nodded her agreement.

The sliding door opened again, and Cooper came back inside, a satisfied expression on his face. "They're interested!" he announced. "Their agent is going to come out tomorrow to have a look."

"Sounds good," Sara said, taking Beth's arm and steering her toward the door. "What time?"

"Eight in the morning." Cooper tucked his papers into a leather bag. "You sleep in at your new place, Beth—I'll handle the viewing. It's better if you're not there."

After saying goodbye, Sara and Beth drove back to the cottage. They found Lily sitting in the garden, her hands folded serenely on her stomach, her eyes closed, her face turned to the sun.

"You're going to get a sunburn, honey," Sara said cheerfully and plopped into a chair.

Lily blinked and smiled. "I like the sun. I'm getting a bit of a tan for once."

"I think I just sold my house." Beth sat down as well, feeling somewhere between stunned and in disbelief she'd really taken it this far.

"Really?" Lily's eyes widened. "That was fast."

"I know." Beth exhaled. "It's a big move for me. Quite literally."

"Congratulations." Lily rose. "Should we celebrate with a cup of tea?"

Beth smiled at the young woman. Beth had accompanied her several times to the cemetery since the funeral, and she seemed glad for Beth's company. Together, they had fallen into a comfortable rhythm of leisurely cooking simple, comforting meals, flipping pancakes in the morning, and grilling barbecue ribs or steaks in the garden at dusk. In between, they went swimming, read books for hours on end, and walked for hours along the coastline to admire the wildflowers and hang their feet into crystal-clear tidepools.

"A cup of tea would be nice," Beth agreed.

Lily went inside smiling, and when the door fell closed behind her, Sara leaned closer. "How does she feel about your move into the cottage?" she whispered. "Is she upset that her mother left it to Ben?"

Beth had been worried about this and brought it up with Lily just the night before. "She was surprised," she shared. "But she didn't expect to inherit it—in fact, she didn't even realize it still belonged to Maggie. And she accepts the fact that her mother wanted Ben to have it. Of course, she also knows she's welcome to stay here whenever she wants."

"You two get along well, don't you?" Sara leaned back, her wicker chair crackling comfortably.

Beth nodded. "She's a lovely person. I wish I could keep her longer. But she wants to get back to her shop in Maine." She drew a deep breath, imagining the empty cottage. "I'll miss her. She's lived with me ever since I moved in. I enjoy the company."

Sara reached over to pat Beth's hand. "I know. But wait and see. Living alone in a place that's all yours is a treat. I love my family, but I adore the rare occasions when I have the house to myself."

Beth smiled and nodded at Sara. Sara was so busy with her job and family that Beth wasn't surprised she longed for a space of her own. But Beth had already had years of it; she knew how it felt to want company and not have it. Once Lily left, she knew she would miss the spark her unexpected guest brought to her life.

"Here's the tea," Lily said just then, carrying a tray with a teapot, cups, and raspberry scones from the farmers market. "There you go." Smiling, she placed it on the table and then poured the tea. "What have you two been talking about?" She handed a cup to Sara and another to Beth. "Me again, was it?" Lily smiled.

"Life," Sara replied. "Specifically, cottage life."

Lily sat back down, crossing her tan legs. Her sandy shorts, faded T-shirt, and sun-bleached tousled bob made her look even younger than she was. "Beth, are you busy preparing for the home sale?" Lily leaned forward, eyes shining.

"Yes, but I've decided to hire a company to do the packing," Beth said and smiled at her guest. "Why?"

"I saw the cutest outfit in a boutique on Mendocino Island," Lily said eagerly. "I would have just bought it for you, but I already had to run to catch the ferry. Maybe we can go back together, do a little shopping?"

"A shopping trip?" Beth tasted the words in her mouth. "Hmm—I'll come for fun, but I have so many clothes already. I should probably go through them now that I'm moving, pick out the keepers." She'd no longer have a large walk-in wardrobe. Only a simple wooden armoire. It was a spacious armoire but fit only a fraction of her outfits.

Lily leaned back, clearly dissatisfied. "If you have so many clothes, why do you always wear the same two things?" she demanded.

Glimpsing the last remnants of a rebellious teenager in the young woman, Beth almost laughed. But the remark hit her too—just like the darts teenage girls fired so expertly. "What do you mean?" She spread out her linen skirt. It was her favorite—the elastic waist was comfy, and pairing it with wide linen blouses was the best defense against sunburn and heat. Plus, her loose attire let Beth forget her ever-expanding hips.

Lily pointed a warning finger at her. "You're hiding in your clothes."

"No, I'm not. I'm not hiding." Beth looked at Sara, who, grinning, shrugged that she was on her own.

"Then why do you never wear anything form-fitting? And I don't mean tight. Just not so ten—so loose."

"Oh." Beth set her cup down. "Were you just about to say tent? Are you saying my clothes are tent-like?"

"No." Lily coughed a laugh away. "No, I would never."

"Frankly, you're drowning in that hippy-dippy blouse and skirt, Bethie," Sara said. "I think the girl's right. Your wardrobe needs a breath of fresh air."

"Well..." A little offended, Beth gathered her skirt and pulled it tight over her legs. "I like hippy-dippy."

Lily suddenly leaned forward, putting a hand on Beth's arm. The laughing spark was gone from her eyes. "Honestly, I was just kidding. You do look great. It was thoughtless of me to comment on your clothes; I really just wanted you to join me on an island shopping spree. I took it too far. I honestly didn't mean what I said."

"No—no." Beth exhaled, trying to get over herself. "You're right, both of you. I've been wearing the same small handful of clothes for too long. I gained a bunch of weight after Ben's death, and most of my things don't fit anymore. I always think I'll starve my way back into them—but it's just not happening."

"Oh, really, you are beautiful the way you are, Beth." Lily sounded so remorseful that Beth had to smile. "I think your generation is too hard on yourselves. I never meant to suggest you should lose weight. Your curves are gorgeous."

Smiling, Beth looked at her rail-thin young guest. "Well, thank you. I do tend to hide them, don't I?"

Lily's eyes brightened. "So—is that a yes?"

Beth laughed. "I already said yes. Let's go shopping this afternoon. Maybe I will find something I like."

"Wish I could join you." Looking envious, Sara rose. "But I have to go."

"I'll walk you to the door," Beth said and followed her friend inside.

Stepping out the front door, Sara turned back. "Lily and you—you sound like mother and daughter."

Beth tilted her head, surprised. "Lily has just lost her mother, Sara. I'm not trying to take that place."

Her friend shrugged. "Aunt, then. You sound like you are Lily's favorite auntie."

"I wish I was her aunt," Beth said after a short pause. "I love that girl already. I wish she could stay longer."

Her face softening, Sara nodded. "Whether you two are related or not doesn't matter, does it?"

Beth's insides stilled. She'd not wanted to ask the grieving girl for information she did not volunteer, poking more sore spots in her soul. "I suppose so," she said quietly. "I still wonder about all that, you know."

Reaching out, Sara wiped a hair from Beth's face. "Of course you wonder, my dear. I think you should come out and ask straight up who her father is. Do it before she leaves. Do it today."

CHAPTER 18

Eager and ready for their shopping spree, Lily skipped the last two stairs, landing on the cheerful new rug in the entryway. For the first time since the funeral, Lily had taken care with her looks, and curling her bob, putting on lipstick, and slipping into pretty clothes felt pretty darn good.

What felt even better was knowing that Mom would be proud of her for picking herself up by her bootstraps.

Tugging on her tank top, her champagne satin skirt fluttering around her knees, Lily joined her host in the middle of the living room. "Do you want to look at anything other than clothes?" Lily asked when she noticed the target of Beth's focus.

"Like what?" Distracted, Beth tapped a finger to her lips.

"Maybe a few sofa pillows," Lily suggested tactfully. The comfy couches were soft and inviting, but they were too bare for her taste. Whenever possible, she gave the furniture she restored a pop of color. "We could also look for some cozy textiles like throw pillows and blankets." Critically, she studied the baby-blue walls. "Frankly, the room could use a fresh coat of paint as well."

Beth tilted her head. "I like blue. It matches the ocean."

"Let's stop by the home goods store. They had a few pretty displays set up when I walked by. Maybe their color palettes inspire us." She grinned, taking Beth's arm. "You, I mean."

Beth sighed, pretending she was put-upon. "Fine. We'll stop by—I need a few new kitchen towels anyway. I ruined most of mine painting the pantry."

"That's a deal then. Wait. Are you going like this?" Lily held Beth at arm's length. While she'd been busy curling her hair, Beth looked like she'd been reading the newspaper, lying on the sofa, and absentmindedly tugging on her hair.

"Yes." Beth glanced down at herself. "I didn't know you'd get all spruced up."

Lily laughed. "You're right. Let's go."

They left, driving Lily's car to the small harbor in Mendocino Cove. It didn't take long for the ferry to arrive, the engine huffing and puffing and smelling of diesel. Snagging seats on the top deck, they were joined by a chatting group of Covians who also seemed set on shopping on the island, armed with empty shopping nets and bags.

Lily waved a greeting at Audrey, the owner of the hotel at Beach and Forgotten, who waved back with a smile. There were several other women with her. Most of them were older, but there were also two women her age, whom Lily would have liked to meet. But Audrey was busy laughing and talking, and Lily didn't want to be awkward and interrupt their merry party.

The ferry ride was beautiful, full of glistening bow waves and white crested wakes, and Beth was enjoying herself so much that Lily forgot all about making new friends. Too soon they arrived and single-filed off the ferry's clattering gangway, stepping safe and sound onto the sun-warmed stones of the island's tiny port.

Lily threaded her arm through Beth's. Breakfast seemed long ago, and suddenly, she felt famished. "How about we start our adventure with iced peach tea and cake?" Without waiting for an answer, she steered Beth away from the screaming gulls that circled a fishing boat bobbing on the waves and toward a row of enticing bakeries and restaurants.

"I might as well if I'm no longer trying to lose this weight." Beth chuckled, but there was a shimmer of guilt in her eyes. Evidently, she still had trouble believing that she truly did look wonderful the way she was.

"You'll walk it right off," Lily promised as she stepped into the café. Before Beth could protest, Lily had already ordered sweet tea with milk and mandarin tartlets topped with freshly whipped cream. They found a sunny table outside with a perfect view of the harbor. The food arrived quickly, which was a relief to Lily—she wasn't sure how much longer she could resist eyeing the chocolate-raspberry torte at the neighboring table.

"I'm so hungry!" Eagerly, she tasted her tartlet, barely bothering to wipe the cream off her lip before taking a second bite. The light, flaky crust melted deliciously in Lily's mouth, and the mandarin slices were perfectly matched with a creamy, airy, sweet but also tart custard that left Lily wishing for more when she was finished.

"Have mine." Beth was trying not to laugh as she pushed her untasted tartlet over. "I'm not hungry."

"Why not?" Lily asked suspiciously, but Beth only laughed more.

"I had a snack while you were getting ready," she admitted. "The leftover lobster roll from last night. I can never resist lobster roll."

"Well, in that case..." Happily, Lily pulled the offered mandarin tartlet over. "I wish I could stay here," she said through a full mouth, barely even recognizing what she was saying until it was too late. Quickly, she swallowed. "Of course, I have to get back to Maine and my store," she said quickly. "I'm looking forward to that too." She'd already imposed on her kind host—she didn't want to seem to be fishing for another invitation to stay longer. At some point, Beth surely would want to enjoy her cottage in peace and quiet.

Beth set down her glass of iced milk tea, wiping the condensation off her fingers with a napkin. "You know I'd like nothing better than to have you stay, Lily."

Lily smiled. "You're so kind to me. I don't deserve it." Her mother had been wonderful, creative, fiercely independent, and always on the go. Nobody would ever replace her in Lily's heart, and she missed her more every day. But Beth was so nurturing and sweet, bringing a calm to Lily's life that was new—and much needed.

"Of course you deserve it, honey. What are you talking about?"

"Nothing." Lily shrugged. "You know...my time here would have been so much harder without you."

"Aww, sweetheart." Beth shook her head, clearly touched. "I'm so glad you stopped by the house the day you arrived."

Agreeing, Lily nodded and then jumped up to bring their tray back inside. "We have shopping to do! Shall we?"

"We shall," Beth declared and rose, pulling a scrunched-up sun hat from her slouchy bag and slapping it unceremoniously on her head.

"We can walk to the shops." Lily pointed at a sandy, winding, inviting path leading into a field of wildflowers and toward the town center. "It'll do us good."

The walk was beautiful, brightened by swaying clusters of white and pink yarrow, lavender seaside daisies and golden poppies, and papery clusters of pearly everlasting and yellow sand verbena. They passed an adorable lighthouse that rose proudly from a garden full of blooming roses, and Beth picked up a brochure about guided tours in passing.

If the walk took a while, Lily hardly noticed, and soon, they reached the small town. Just for fun, they first strolled along the famous Wedding Lane with all its bridal shops, admiring the gorgeous gowns and sparkling jewels on display. The sun was already dipping toward the sea when they finally reached the small boutique Lily remembered.

Lily sensed Beth's mix of excitement and hesitation when she stepped into the pretty store.

CHAPTER 19

L ook at this!" Lily immediately guided her to a rack by the window and showed her a flowy wrap dress.

"Oh." Unsure, Beth felt the coral-colored fabric. "That's different. I usually just wear earth tones. Brown and moss green, sand...that sort of thing."

Lily was well aware. "But this would look so good with your skin tone," she coaxed. "Plus, it'll make your eyes pop." At work, she dealt daily with tones, hues, and fabrics. Her trained eye had immediately identified the most flattering palette for Beth, and it didn't include moss green. With her clear skin and luscious lips, Beth reminded Lily of a vintage film star. Instead of hiding her enviable curves, accentuating them would turn Beth into a brunette Brigitte Bardot.

"Okay." Beth accepted the dress, looking unconvinced. "Trying it on won't hurt."

The salesperson, a woman Beth's age or a bit older, had caught the words. Her eyes met Lily's, and she gave a discreet thumbs-up.

"That's the spirit," Lily said bracingly, returning her attention to Beth. "Look, it's a super comfortable wrap dress—it ties at the waist. They have it in blue too."

"I do like wraps. It's been forever since I wore one." A spark of interest moved over Beth's features as she added the blue wrap to the coral.

"And what about this?" Lily went to another rack, where a sunny yellow blouse caught her eye. It had a broad strip of white hand embroidery around the neckline, which would add a cheerful glimpse of tan skin. Lily held the blouse up to Beth. "Ooh. It makes you look so radiant! Definitely this one. Wear it with capris and your wedge espadrilles, and you'll look like Sophia Loren."

"If you think so." Doubtful but resigned, Beth added it to the dresses. "I might as well try it on."

"Can I start you a fitting room with these?" The salesperson stepped forward, smiling. She was one of those women who seemed born to work in a boutique—friendly, full of energy, and effortlessly stylish with her black page cut and bright patterned blouse.

"Yes, please, uh—" Beth looked up.

"Agnes," the woman filled the expectant pause. "My name is Agnes."

"I'm Beth." Turning, she handed Agnes the clothes. "Um, wait, maybe..." She picked a pair of high-waist-ed linen pants in a soft cream shade from the rack beside her. "I like these." She held them up to the yellow blouse. "They go with it, don't they?"

"Absolutely. I also just bought a pair of those," Agnes supported the choice. "They are incredibly comfort-able, and they flow down to the ankles. Very chic. I pair them with this shirt. Have a look." She nodded at a navy linen shirt short enough to show off the waist.

"I like that shirt," Beth admitted. While her hips seemed to grow with every lobster roll, her small waist was her secret pride. "I like it in white too."

"Great choice." Spotting the same colors among the pants still on the rack, Lily rifled through the hangers until she found matching blue pants. "I'd get a pair in white and blue for each shirt and pants," she suggested. "Between these, you can get a lot of great combinations and never even have to think about it."

Beth laughed and held up a hand to make Lily stop pulling out more clothes. "Let me try this on first," she said, following Agnes. "Maybe none of it fits. Also fair warning, Lily—I'm used to elastic waists and might want to stay with my trusted skirts."

"You look like a retired librarian in them," Lily said heartlessly.

"And what's wrong with that?" Beth countered cheerfully. "Retired librarians are the best people in the world."

Lily laughed, caught out. "You're right. I'll shut up now."

While Beth was trying on her new clothes, Lily and Agnes also found a long, soft, knitted cardigan in a sweet dove-gray color that was perfect for breezy evenings in the garden and foggy mornings when Beth had coffee on the steps to the beach, and a flattering, ruched, one-piece swimsuit in sea-glass green.

Watching Beth try on the clothes was like witnessing a long-buried light slowly flicker back to life. Seeing her friend's face when Beth stepped out of the dressing room in the coral wrap dress made Lily's heart swell. Beth paused in front of the mirror, her hand resting nervously on her stomach, but there was something different in her eyes—an almost forgotten glimmer of confidence. The way the dress clung to her curves made her look softer, maybe even fuller, but in the most beautiful way.

"You look amazing," Lily said, her voice full of genuine awe. Beth turned, her cheeks flushing. "I haven't worn anything this colorful in a while."

Lily gave a playful shrug. "It suits you. You look like you're ready to conquer the world."

"Really?" Beth returned to her image in the mirror.

"Spit twice and die, Beth. I promise. You are gorgeous."

"Um. Well, I think it's a yes for me too. Should I try on the blue one too?" Beth asked eagerly.

"Absolutely." Lily smiled, touched.

Each new outfit Beth tried on seemed to melt away another layer of doubt. The yellow tunic? She beamed putting it on, her shoulders lifting as if the embroidery had wiped away a decade of grief. The linen pants? Lily couldn't stop grinning when Beth twirled in front of the mirror, letting the material fly. And when Beth tried on the swimsuit, Lily had to bite her lip to hold back a cheer. Beth stood straighter, her reflection showing a woman who was ready to dive back into life.

By the time they brought the pile of clothes to the register, Beth's face was glowing with a kind of shy joy. "I haven't looked this good in ages," she declared.

Lily smiled. "Now you're seeing what everyone else does—how beautiful you are."

At the checkout counter, Agnes greeted them with a huge smile. "Great choices!" she chirped, picking up the items Beth laid out. "This dress sits great on you! And these pants—you're going to love how breezy they are." Beth smiled, still not quite used to the attention, but Lily could see that the compliments were starting to sink in. "You've got super taste," Agnes added as she folded the tunic neatly. "And I don't just say that to everyone."

"Thanks." Beth smiled at Lily. "I had a little help."

Agnes grinned. "Well, that's what daughters are for, aren't they? And can I just say, it's wonderful to see women help each other embrace their beauty."

"Thank you," Beth murmured, flushing with pleasure and glancing at Lily, who smiled back that it wasn't necessary to correct the mistake about their relationship.

After ringing them up, Agnes handed the bags over. "You ladies enjoy the rest of your day. And remember, life's too short to wear boring clothes!"

As they left the boutique, Beth walked lighter. Lily knew it wasn't just the clothes that had changed—it was the way Beth felt about herself.

Chapter 20

Strolling down the sunny street, their arms full of shopping bags, Lily caught sight of something in a nearby shop. "Beth, look," she said, her eyes widening with appreciation as she pulled her companion toward an old, slightly rundown antique store.

In the dusty window sat the most charming reading chair Lily had ever seen. She stepped closer, drawn to the gleam of the warm wood that was visible even through the blind, salt-etched glass. The faded upholstery was worn and frayed, but the frame—an elegant, curved design—still seemed sturdy. The way it sat there, the faded floral pattern warming in the afternoon sunlight, made Lily want to climb in, pull up her feet, and curl into a cozy ball.

"It's pretty." Beth sounded almost surprised. "You like it, huh?"

Lily nodded, unable to tear her eyes away. It was the time of day and weather to play volleyball on the beach or go swimming or visit the botanical garden and eat pistachio ice cream in a waffle cone, not curl up in a comfy chair at home. But while she couldn't pinpoint what exactly drew her to the chair, it did pluck a string deep inside her heart. "It's the perfect reading chair. Can't you just see yourself sitting in it on a rainy day with a good book and a cat on your lap?"

"I have a cat allergy." Beth raised an eyebrow. "The chair is lovely...but a little worse for wear, don't you think?" She wrinkled her nose as if she could smell musty upholstery.

Lily smiled. "A little work and it could be perfect—we all deserve a second chance, don't we? Chairs included." Without a second thought, Lily pulled Beth inside the shop. The interior was cluttered, filled with old furniture, knick-knacks, and the smell of aged wood and dried oil paint. A bell tinkled as the door swung shut behind them.

"Well, hello." Behind the counter, like a spectacled Santa Claus, sat a big man with wiry white hair and thick glasses perched on his nose. He had a soft, wrinkled face and an air of quiet contentment. Peering at them near-sightedly, he stroked his long beard.

"Hello," Beth said, hitching her shopping bags higher. "We've, uh..."

"Hi," Lily said brightly. She liked the old man. His contentment felt contagious. "Can we have a look at the reading chair in the window?"

"Hmm. Oh." He turned to her, squinting to see better. "Well, since it isn't Maggie, it must be little Lily Porter," he finally said, his voice as old as the wood surrounding him. Pushing his glasses higher on his nose, he gave her a knowing smile. "Looks like you're all done growing up."

"You know me?" Lily stopped short.

"You're the spitting image of your mother."

Lily blinked in surprise. "You knew my mom?"

The man chuckled like creaking floorboards. "Oh, I knew her well. Maggie used to come in here all the time, browsing for little treasures and helping my wife out. This chair you're looking at? She loved it. Sat in it more than once when she was expecting you and a fair few times after."

Lily's heart skipped a beat. "She did?" She walked over to the chair and ran her fingers over the worn fabric. Was that the reason she'd been so drawn to it? Was it a connection to a past she barely remembered?

Beth came to stand beside her. "It is a nice chair, Lily," she murmured.

Lily looked at the shopkeeper, something stirring in her chest. "Did my mom ever talk about—about my father?" she asked, her voice hesitant. Despite her questions, Mom had never told Lily about him. Trying to respect Mom's choices—since there really was no other way of dealing with them—Lily rarely allowed herself to think about her father. But now, the chair opened a door she didn't know she needed to step through.

"You don't know who your father is?" Lily registered Beth's tense whisper but didn't quite process it.

"The only thing I know is that they met in Mendocino," Lily replied softly, glancing at Beth before turning back to the man. "Did she tell you about him?"

He raised an eyebrow as if he was surprised to learn she didn't know her father, and it took him a long moment to reply. "It's been a while since I talked to Maggie. She stopped coming when my wife got sick."

"Mom passed away recently too," Lily said. "I live in Maine and only came back to Mendocino Beach to bury her next to my grandparents."

He shook his head with regret. "I'm sorry to hear that. I'd have come to the funeral had I known, but I don't read the newspaper, and I rarely leave the store anymore. But I'd have liked the chance to say good-bye to a friend." The man's expression softened, and he leaned on the counter. "Hmm. Your mother was a private young woman, but she did let slip a few things to my wife now and then. My wife shared everything with me; at least I like to think she did. I miss her." He sighed. "Since you're asking...there's something I remember."

Lily's breath caught in her throat. She nodded, her hand still resting on the chair. "What can you tell me?"

The man glanced around as if to make sure they were alone. "Your father and Maggie were high school sweethearts, dating in their senior year." He smiled wistfully. "A stormy first love it was, my wife said, full of kisses and fights and gym dances. Toward the end of the year, Maggie began to sneak out to meet him at the beach at night. My wife said the two of them gave each other secret tutoring lessons." He looked significantly over the rim of his glasses, making sure Lily caught his meaning. "I thought they were much too young. My wife tried to talk to her, but Maggie wasn't one for taking advice, even if it was well-meant." He shrugged. "Of course it all came out in the end. Your grandma was none too happy. But Maggie still came to sit in the chair."

"Did my father end it?" Lily sounded hoarse.

"Oh, he was head over heels. As far as he was concerned, she was the one." The old man stroked his beard, his gaze turned inward as he remembered the past. "The thing was, he was set on going to a certain university—I don't remember where, but it was far away. Maybe it was Boston? I don't remember, but I know she wasn't ready to give up her life here to follow him into a big city. The thing is, that was before she realized she was...you know." He winked at Lily.

"Oh," Beth whispered. "Oh."

He turned to look at her, a puzzled expression crossing his face before he turned back to Lily. "Those kids broke their hearts when they split up, only they didn't realize it." He stroked his beard. "Next thing we knew, he was dating a new girl while Maggie was still trying to figure out what she wanted to do. By the time she'd made up her mind, he was engaged to his consolation prize. My wife always said he tied that poor little gal down before she could run too. But my wife was sure he never got over Maggie. First love hurts the worst, and that's the truth."

Beth abruptly set her shopping bags on the ground, hugging herself as if she was cold. She looked pale. "Do you remember his name?"

"Um..." The old man pulled out a tissue, taking his time shaking it out and blowing his nose as he tried to remember. "Benny...Thomas. No—Thompson. Yeah, that's right, Benny Thompson. Besides taking it too far with Maggie, he sounded like a pretty good kid. Full of plans, with a knack for drawing. Loyal until she cut him loose, and real generous." He chuckled. "So generous that he gave Maggie something to remember him by—you." He nodded at Lily.

"Me." The simple, small word set off a mix of emotions in her—shock, sadness, but also a strange, otherworldly sense of completion. She wasn't sure what to say, but it felt like a missing piece of her identity had just been returned to her. "Ben was my dad." The name sounded like the chair looked—oddly familiar, as if their memory had been Lily's all along.

Beth's sharp intake of breath at her side made her take a step back. Of course...Ben Thompson. He'd been Beth's husband.

"Don't take it personally if he wasn't in your life, honey." The shopkeeper spread his hands as if to apologize for her father's absence. "Maggie was spitting mad that he moved on so quickly. She swore never to tell him about you. Besides, her mom swore he would come and claim you for himself, whisking you away from Mendocino. My wife and I thought differently, but it wasn't our business to meddle. Besides, that's when my wife got sick... Her treatment was all I could think about. Maggie stopped coming soon after, seeing that my wife barely had energy for visits and all that." A faraway look glazed his eyes. "But I've wondered about Maggie and her baby over the years. Wish I could've talked to her one more time."

Beth placed a hand on her arm. "You okay, Lily?" Her voice sounded strained.

Lily nodded before noticing the trembling of Beth's hand. "Yeah, I think I am. Are you?"

"Of course," Beth said, the words dripping too slowly from her lips. "It was before he and—he didn't know. I didn't know."

"Seems only Mom and Grandma knew." Her mind racing, Lily took Beth's hand and squeezed before letting go again. A secret sign—they were going to talk, work through it, tackle the secrets of the past together. Then, Lily turned to the shopkeeper. She needed something real and practical to hold on to. "I want to buy the chair."

His eyes twinkled. "I thought you might. It's yours for a fair price. And...if you ever want to talk more about your mother, you know where to find me."

Moving inside a cloud of cotton muffling reality, Lily paid a pittance for the chair, not even realizing he was practically gifting it to her. When she signed the receipt, Beth, busy gathering the shopping bags she'd dropped, cleared her throat. "Where are you going to put it?"

"Oh." Lily capped the pen and pushed the signed slip across the counter. "Right. I hadn't even thought about it." She felt so much at home in the little seaside cottage; she'd missed the part where the chair was in Mendocino and she lived in Maine.

"If you want a refund, it's not a problem." The old man put a hand on the receipt, ready to return it.

"No," Beth said determinedly. "Thank you. But she's going to take it." She turned to Lily. "Keep it at the cottage. Put it in your bedroom or make it that pop of color you were looking for in the living room. If you want it shipped to Maine—then shipping is on me. I want you to have that chair."

"Really?" Shipping would be too expensive, but Lily loved the idea of keeping her chair in the cottage better, anyway. A connection to her past as much as a plan for the future.

Beth smiled, a tight smile but genuine. "I don't think it was by accident that you spotted it in the window, sweetheart. I think your mom wants you to have it."

"That's... I truly appreciate it, Beth." Lily put a hand to her heart. The old man's revelation affected Beth as much as Lily or more... She reached out, taking a couple of the shopping bags to relieve Beth. "I'll have to mess around restoring it. Are you sure I can do that at the cottage?"

"Yes, of course. If you weed your way through to that little shed, you can turn it into your workshop." Beth smiled, the corners of her mouth relaxing. "I just want you to be happy, sweetheart." She turned to the shopkeeper. "Can you deliver to my place in Mendocino Beach? I'm happy to pay for the service."

He smiled his creaky smile. "No need for payment. I also want our little girl here to have her mom's chair." He chuckled. "Just write down your address for me." He pushed a sepia notepad over and pulled a pencil from behind his ear. "I'll be over there next week in the truck anyway, seeing the good doctor for my diabetes. I'll stop by after and drop off the chair, see how Maggie's girl is doing."

"That would be great. Text me before you leave, and I'll make sure to have coffee and cake for the occasion." Beth scribbled down her phone number and address. "Thanks."

"Thank you." Lily held out her hand to the old man. "I'm sorry—in all the excitement, I missed your name."

"Never said it." He shook her hand, holding it in both of his. "But it's Henry. Henry Oblinger."

"Of course it is." She smiled. "It was wonderful meeting you, Henry."

"That's how I feel too." Grinning, he leaned onto the counter. "You've got yourself a good grip there."

"I restore furniture for a living. I need a good grip."

"Look at that." His grin spread to his eyes. "Here I thought I was the only upholsterer on the island. Maybe you and I will turn out to be kindred spirits, Lily."

"Maybe. Bye—we'll see you next week." She slipped her free arm under Beth's, and they left, looking back to see Henry stroking his beard thoughtfully.

They'd only taken a few steps down the sunny lane when Beth suddenly teetered, almost losing her balance. "Oh," she said and dropped a bag, putting the hand to her forehead as if she was going to faint. "Oh, no."

Taking Beth's arm more firmly, Lily guided her into the shade of a nearby oak. "I know," she said softly. The cottony cloud was lifting for both her and her friend. "We are almost related, aren't we? It's just hitting me now too."

Beth turned to her, her eyes shimmering. "Ben had no idea," she whispered. "We didn't have kids. He would have been over the moon to learn you exist."

"I don't know if that's true." Lily inhaled. If he'd wanted, Ben could have easily found Maggie and her... "But I do know another thing for sure: you never were a consolation prize." Lily hugged Beth until her shoulders relaxed, and Beth hugged her back. "Mom often said she was glad she never married. I knew her—I know she was telling the truth. She really was glad. And if he'd really loved her so much, he'd have come looking for her. No." She shook her head, a little sad, a little relieved. "He loved you."

"You think?" Beth whispered. "Are you sure?"

"Absolutely."

"What about the beach house? Why would she give it to Ben?"

"Who knows." Lily shrugged. "Maybe she wanted to bring him back to Mendocino too? Maybe it was her way to introduce him to me."

Or maybe, Ben had been the love of Maggie's life even if he broke her heart, and she'd wanted him to have the house of their memories. It didn't matter now.

Lily couldn't change the past. She couldn't get back that childhood with two loving parents she'd longed for. But she could make the future a little easier, a little kinder for her friend.

Inhaling the salty air that smelled of ocean and beach daisies, old love and new beginnings, she let the corners of her lips curve into her brightest smile. "I promise you, Beth—Ben belonged to you. You were the love of his life."

CHAPTER 21

It was early in the morning; fog still hung thick in the sandy lanes, muting the first rays of sunlight into veils of gold. Alex had not yet come down from the apartment.

Staring in the mirror of the little bathroom in the back of the bookstore, Hannah nervously tucked her hairbrush back in her tote. Her hand shook a little touching up her lipstick, and she overlined her cupid's bow. Muttering under her breath, she tore off a piece of toilet paper and wiped the lipstick off again.

Bracing her hands on the sink, she lowered her head and took a breath. Her nerves fluttered like moths in her chest.

He had been out of touch since walking away on the beach two days ago. Warm cinnamon rolls had kept appearing on her patio table, but Hannah didn't know if her breakfast was due to his love or his sense of duty.

She straightened, tilting her head as she caught a sound. A door scraped. Then, steps lightly descended the wooden stairs outside, and she could hear whistling. A song—*You are my sunshine*. Trying to control the scary fluttering in her chest, she cast a last glance into the mirror and hurried back into the store, leaning against the counter to steady herself.

Hopefully, he had forgiven her for bringing up their living arrangement so awkwardly. Hopefully, he would want to simply resume where they'd left off before she put her foot in her mouth.

The door opened, and Alli appeared, baby Tommy in her arms. "Ah!" Startled, she jerked back, clutching Tommy to her chest. Then, she started laughing. "Hannah! What are you doing here?"

Despite her disappointment, Hannah smiled. It was hard not to, seeing the rosy-cheeked pair. "Can I?" She held out her arms.

"Anytime." Readily, Alli handed over the cooing bundle. "Another good night," she reported proudly. "For both of us."

"He's such a good baby." Hannah kissed Tommy's soft, sweet-smelling cheek and was rewarded with a gurgle and an eager spit-bubble. She started swaying to keep him happy. "Hey, I thought you two were still in San Francisco." Saying the words, she realized what it meant. If Alli had spent the night in the little apartment over the bookstore—where was Alex?

"Yes, well." Alli hopped up on the counter, crossing her legs. "Turns out my mother brought her new man to live with her. Only she didn't mention it to me, in case I wouldn't come."

"I see." Hannah nodded. "Third wheel, huh?"

"Definitely third wheel," Alli confirmed. "Also, I missed the sea. There's something special about stepping out of your door in the morning and getting hit by that cold, clammy, salty breeze." She chuckled, pointing over her shoulder at the golden fog outside the shop window. "Don't want to miss it anymore."

"I know." Hannah tried to smile. "So—where's Alex?"

"Oh." Alli's eyes widened with surprise. "I thought he was staying with you?"

"Um. No." Tommy squawked, making Hannah realize she was holding him too tight. Quickly, she loosened her grip and resumed her swaying. "The last I heard of him was that he wanted to talk with you about moving back into the apartment."

Alli jumped down. "I never heard from him, Hannah. Does he want the apartment back?"

"I'm not sure." Hannah's thoughts raced.

"Did you two have a fight?" Alli gently took Tommy from her.

"Not...sure either." Hannah inhaled. "I don't really know what happened. I wanted to talk about our living arrangements. I don't want him to feel trapped staying at my house, so I suggested he move back—"

"You said that?" Alli interrupted, aghast.

"No!" Hannah held up her hands before dropping them. "Not like that, at least."

"The man is head over heels for you," Alli said gently. "And now he thinks he overstayed his welcome."

"The man has lived alone for most of his life," Hannah said reasonably. "Was it so bad to want to make sure he's got his space?"

"Of course not." Alli pulled out her silk sling from under the counter, expertly wrapping it around her and the baby. "I mean, it depends on how you say it. But don't worry—I'm sure it takes more than that to put Alex off." She smiled at Hannah.

"Why am I so nervous then?"

"Because you had a bad marriage," Alli said wisely. She and Hannah had talked about lots of things when they lived together after Evan left them. "That stuff leaves scars. You're doing your best. But Alex is the most stable guy I know. You should trust him to tell you when he needs space. He's not like Evan, who went out and started a second family. Most men aren't. At least, I hope."

"I only want Alex to be happy," Hannah said weakly. "And now he doesn't answer my texts."

Alli glanced around as if she was looking for the man in question between the tall bookshelves. But there were only books and comfy chairs and tiny dust motes swirling in the brightening light of the morning. "He doesn't answer your texts? That seems strange."

"He's gone on another job, isn't he?" Hannah bit her lip. It was what she'd feared even more than a senseless fight. He'd been called away again, exposing himself to who knew what dangers.

"Maybe he's just visiting a friend?" Alli suggested, her voice unconvinced.

"He'd answer my texts if he could." Hannah sank against the counter. "I should've known! I was so caught up in my own stupid little drama." The moths in her chest folded their nervous wings, dropping like hard little pebbles of fear on her stomach. She pressed a hand to it. "I don't have a good feeling about this, Alli."

Alli folded her hands to make a suggestion. "Let's have a nice, calm cup of tea," she decided. "I have to go get Tommy's bottle ready anyway."

"What about the store?" Hannah's sense of duty kicked in. The front door creaked open, chiming the little bell.

"Forget about the store," Alli said resolutely, too busy tying the sling to catch the small sound. "It's not like the buyers are kicking in our doors. Nobody will notice if we lock up and go have a cup of tea."

"I'll notice," a deep voice said.

CHAPTER 22

Hannah whisked around. "Alex!"

"Hey, baby." He grinned at her, tan and handsome and starry-eyed as ever. "I missed you."

"I missed you too!" She hurried around the counter, all obsessing and worrying forgotten. "I'm so sorry I said we needed to slow down! I'm so glad you're back!" She threw herself into his arms, not caring whether he was ready to catch her.

"Ooh. Oof." Catching her with only one arm, he laughed but flinched, letting her down gently instead of pulling her into his usual bear hug.

"What? What is that?" She jumped back, taking his hands and spreading his arms to inspect him.

"Nothing." He pulled her back to him. "It's nothing."

"It's something." She wiggled free again, taking hold of his shirt hem and lifting it. "You're all wrapped up! What is this? What happened?" A white bandage wound around his chest, and purple bruising spread where the skin was visible.

Even Alli, still standing by the counter, gasped.

He took Hannah's hands into his, making her drop the shirt. "I was shot at," he whispered so only she could hear. "But they missed."

"Oh no." Hannah's stomach dropped. "I thought you said you were safe!"

"Uh—I'm going upstairs to make that tea. Whenever you two are ready." Looking alarmed, Alli hurried out of the door, leaving them alone in the store.

"Sit down." Hannah guided Alex to one of the cozy armchairs and sank onto the matching footstool.

His face looked like it was hewn from a block of granite as he lowered himself into the chair. It must've hurt, but he didn't blink once. "I think I'm bleeding," he declared stoically after a while, gingerly lifting his shirt to check. To Hannah's relief, the bandage was just as pristine as before. He dropped the shirt again and grinned. "False alarm. Good—I like this shirt."

"Heavens," Hannah said weakly. "What happened? You have to tell me, Alex."

"Um..." Despite clearly being in pain, his eyes glittered with laughter. "Well, I can't, sweetheart."

"But—" she protested before he cut her off.

"It's only a flesh wound," he said, leaning back and closing his eyes. "The bullet grazed me. It'll heal. They stitched me up good. It'll be alright."

"How can you say that?" Hannah demanded, her shock morphing into anger. "You're putting your life in danger every time you go out there!"

He opened his eyes, holding her gaze. "They saw me."

Her anger evaporated as quickly as it had come, wiped out by confusion. Hannah took his hand into hers. "They saw you? What does that mean? Who are they? Does that mean they'll come after you?"

"They don't know my real identity, nor are they going to find out," Alex reassured her in a low, calm voice. "It's a lot of effort down the drain. But there's the bright side."

"What does that mean?" Hope lifted Hannah's heart despite the emotions swirling in her head, making it hard to think.

"It means I'm no longer useful to the mission." He smiled, flipping his hand so he was holding hers. His hand was large and warm, his grip confident. "It means I'm done. From now on, I'm just a bookseller."

"It's over? For real?" She rose, holding his starry gaze. Could she believe him?

His grin was genuine, relaxed despite the pain he must be in. "For real, Hannah. I might have to train someone now and then—but that's no problem. A vacation, really."

Swallowing her ebbing worries, Hannah asked, "You're going to stay in Mendocino Beach now?"

"I was hoping you'd like the news." He picked up a curl, playing with it. "Also strikes me as lucky I get to stick around and watch morale. Shutting down the store in the middle of the day to drink tea and such..." He clucked his tongue, but his fingers tucked the curl behind her ear, tenderly tracing the curve of her neck."

"That was just because I was so worried about you." She leaned against his knee, enjoying the delicious way his touch electrified her skin.

"I like it when you worry about me." His grin deepened.

Half-heartedly, she swatted at his shin. "No, you don't. It feels terrible." To her surprise, her vision started to swim. She wiped it away, shaking her head and trying to laugh, but it came out more like a sob as the rollercoaster of her feelings took another turn.

"Hey. Hey. Come here." Alex rose, pulling her with him. He wrapped his arms around her waist, pulling her in on his good side for a long, sweet kiss. "I meant to call you to let you know I had to leave that night, but they were already at my door to pick me up. I'm sorry."

She kissed him back. "But you're done with everything now," she confirmed one more time when she had to come up for air.

"Not with you, babe," he murmured, his starry gaze burning her cheeks. "I'm only getting started here. Oh. Ouch." He winced, his face distorting for a moment before he caught himself.

"Careful, Alex." Hannah stepped away. "Or it'll really start bleeding."

"Whatever. I...ugh." He narrowed his eyes, gingerly pressing a hand to the wound. "I wasn't going to let it keep me from all the things I wanted to do to you, but..."

"But you don't want to bleed all over me. Thank you, honey." She reached up with a smile, sweeping his hair back.

"Mmm—yeah," he growled, catching her hand and kissing her palm. "Just trying to keep you safe."

Laughing, Hannah took another step back. "I'll bring the car to the front. I'm taking you to the cottage to take care of you."

"That sounds wonderful, nurse. I need you to take care of me." He started to kiss the inside of her wrist, his hungry lips quickly moving higher, but she pulled away her arm and raised a warning finger.

"Strictly medical and mental care only, until all wounds are healed," she declared, laughing again when he groaned in protest and slipping from his grip.

"Come back," he demanded, but even though there was nothing she wanted more, Hannah only blew him a kiss and left to get her car and bring her hero home.

CHAPTER 23

Leaning on her spade, Beth glanced up at the sky. "Looks like it's going to rain. How strange—the forecast called for blue skies."

"That's a welcome surprise then," Mateo replied, turning his gaze to the ocean. "It's been too dry. We really need the rain."

"But right now? We're about to plant your olive tree!" For the past three weeks, they'd enjoyed sunshine in the afternoons. Now, choppy waves curled and crashed as a rising wind forced Beth to grip her gardening hat tightly.

"Good! That's perfect weather for planting trees!" Mateo promised and stepped on the spade to drive the blade into the ground. "It won't take long. We'll be back inside before it starts raining."

She laughed. "How do you know how long it takes? You said you've never planted a tree before!" They'd met at the farmers market in the morning, and he asked after the little tree he'd gifted her. When she told him she thought the pot would be too small soon, he'd offered to come and put it in the ground for her. Beth gladly accepted the offer—and resigned herself to the happy blush warming her cheeks for all to see.

They had met several times since their dinner on the beach, and each encounter had been more pleasant and lovely than the last. Mateo was a natural nurturer; he took genuine pleasure in caring for people, often anticipating Beth's needs before she even realized them.

And even though she was more attracted to him than ever, she was grateful he hadn't kissed her goodnight when he walked her home along the shore.

Beth had learned that Mateo wasn't interested in a quick, half-drunken kiss—he'd had plenty of those in his life. "They do nothing for me," he had said one day, laughing when she mentioned a kissing scene on TV. "My heart is ready for love."

When she turned to him, the intensity of his dark gaze on her made her blush even more than the anticipation of his tree-planting visit...

"You're asking me how long it takes to plant a tiny tree like this?" Mateo shrugged in that effortless way only Italians could. "Not long. How hard can it be?"

Sliding into the soil, the spade hit something solid. He muttered under his breath, scraping away the layer of soil he'd disturbed. "A rock," he said, frowning as he worked to dig it out. With a wide arc, he tossed the rock into the ocean, watching it splash into the waves.

Beth smiled. "Is it hard to dig?" she asked as the spade stopped short again.

"No." He grinned, bending to dig out this stone as well. "Not for real men like me. A real man can dig a hole anywhere." The stone hit the waterline, and Mateo philosophically leaned on the handle to watch until the waves swallowed it.

"Oh, good." Beth was about to giggle when the spade hit another rock in the sandy soil, but a sudden gust ripped the laughter from her lips. She squeezed her eyes shut, and before she'd opened them again, raindrops started falling on her face.

Driven by the wild force of wind and sea, the raindrops were big, fat, and surprisingly cold.

"Oh!" The hem of her new wrap dress fluttered well above her knees. Laughing, Beth tugged it down, feeling like a coastal, dark-haired Marilyn Monroe. "We could finish this another time, Mateo!" she called over the growling sea.

As if nature had just waited for the words, the storm intensified. The rain went from fat droplets to sheets, drenching them instantly. Beth crossed her arms over her chest, suddenly aware of how translucent the fabric had become. The dress was light, and while she had splurged on a chic new bra since her island shopping trip, it certainly wasn't meant to be seen—at least not like this...

"The hole is almost big enough! We can do it! We can do anything we want, Bella!" Mateo flung a spadeful of dirt to the side and dug in again. The wind pressed his soaked linen shirt against his torso, tugging at his hair. Suddenly, he laughed triumphantly and held out a hand for the tree.

"Is it deep enough?" Beth had to yell to make herself heard over the roar of Poseidon's rising seafoam horses. The waves galloped wildly onto the beach, crashing into the sand with breakers as fierce as iron-shod hooves.

Mateo glanced at the ocean and gestured for Beth to drop the root ball into the hole. The little tree landed a little haphazardly, and he quickly scraped the soil back around it. "The first time you do something new, it's always perfect!" he called over the natural cacophony surrounding them. "Did you know?"

"No!" she called back. "I thought it was the other way around—the first time is never perfect!"

"How can it be, if it's new to you?" Mateo shook his head, stamping the soil down. "If it's a bit crooked, a bit messy—that just makes it more beautiful!"

She laughed, distracted by the cold rain running down her neck. "If you say so!"

Tossing the spade aside, he grabbed Beth's hand, and together they started running toward the house.

Laughing so hard she thought she might stitch her side, Beth leaned against the kitchen counter. The sudden chaos of everything—the storm, the crooked planting, the soaked new dress—had unleashed something within her.

"Funny, eh?" Mateo shook the water off his hands and leaned against the closed door, his back pressed against it.

"Yeah." She giggled until the fire burning in his eyes made her stop.

"So, you enjoy gardening with me?" There was a new undercurrent to his voice—wilder and more passionate than before.

"Mateo," she whispered.

"Is the kid at home?" His dark eyes flicked to the door and back to her as if his gaze couldn't survive with the sight of her.

Beth dropped her arms, defenseless. "She's gone to meet her new friends at the hotel at Beach and Forgotten."

Mateo took a step toward her, running his fingers through his hair. "We are alone, my beautiful?"

Heart fluttering with the force of a thousand hummingbirds, Beth moistened her lips. He was impossibly handsome with his silver-streaked, rain-wet curls and those eyes that belonged absolutely, utterly, to her. "We are alone."

"I want you," he murmured, closing the distance between them. He reached out to wipe a wet strand of hair plastered to her face back where it belonged, his hand continuing to trail gently down her cheek. Beth's breath caught as his fingers brushed her skin, leaving fire in their wake despite the chill clinging to them from the rain. Her heart raced as Mateo's gaze deepened, his dark eyes intense yet tender, searching hers for any hint of hesitation.

There was none. After years of holding herself back and denying her desires, Beth felt the barriers she'd built begin to crumble. She didn't care about the translucent dress or the storm raging outside; she cared about this moment, about him.

"I've wanted this too," she admitted softly, the words slipping out before she could second-guess herself. Her voice trembled with a mixture of excitement and nervousness, yet beneath it all was clarity—a tide pulling her toward something inevitable and wonderful.

Mateo's lips curved into a slow, knowing smile. He brought both hands to her waist, the heat of his touch spreading through the soaked fabric of her dress. "Then let me show you, Beth," he whispered, his voice barely audible over the sound of rain pattering against the windows. "Let me show you how good it can be."

Beth nodded, her body moving toward him, drawn by his magnetic force. Her arms slipped around his neck, the feel of his damp curls under her fingers strangely grounding in the almost otherworldly moment that broke her shell, catapulting her out of her comfort zone and into something new and wild and dangerous. He pulled her closer, their bodies pressing together, the warmth between them a sharp contrast to the cold rain dripping from their clothes.

Mateo's breath brushed her ear, her cheek, her neck as his hands traced her curves. "You are so beautiful, Beth," he murmured, his low voice sending shivers down her spine.

She exhaled, feeling a thrill rush through her. Ben had loved her, but she had never felt this desired. Beth closed her eyes, letting the hesitant widow slip away, a persona that suddenly felt like a heavy mantle, a burden, a hair shirt she had never wanted to wear.

Her hands slid to his chest, feeling the steady thrum of his heartbeat under the soaked shirt. Mateo kissed her, gently at first, testing the waters, checking if she was ready, if she was giving herself freely. It was sweet and slow, but she already felt the hunger below, a fiery promise of more.

Kissing him back, giving him the permission he needed, she curled her fingers into his hair. The only thing she could hear was the sound of their breath mingling, of her heart beating for him. Pulling back just enough to meet her eyes, Mateo smiled. "You're even more stunning when you let go, Beth," he murmured, his voice husky with longing. "Don't ever hide from me who you really are."

"I won't," she promised, leaning into his warmth, into his safety and passion. Fully and truly alive for the first time since forever, she was ready to embrace every crooked, messy, beautiful moment ahead.

CHAPTER 24

B eth set her phone on the table and looked up at the grapevine groves that covered the gently sloping hills surrounding the winery. As if to make amends for the thunderstorm the night before, a playful, warm breeze carried the scents of sweet grapes and sun-warmed oak trees.

"Everything okay?" Lily smiled over her steaming coffee cup at Beth. "You have that faraway come-hither look again. Did anything interesting happen while I was out last night?" She'd accepted an invitation to a night out with Audrey, Zoe, and a couple of their friends.

"Uh, I do not have a come-hither look, missy. How was last night? Where did you go?" Clearing her throat, Beth snapped back to the present, quickly picking up her own mug to hide behind it. The things that had happened the night before still drove warm blood to her cheeks if she allowed herself to indulge in the constant flashbacks popping up in front of her inner eye. Luckily, Mateo left just before Lily returned, and Beth had already—still—been in bed, not meeting her guest until the next morning when the young woman suggested the breakfast buffet at the Mendocino Cove winery.

"Nah-ah," Lily said, squinting to see Beth better. "We're talking about you. You're blushing. What are you—ah. Ahaaa." She leaned back, grinning. "It's Mateo, isn't it? Did he—did you and he finally—"

Beth set down her cup, a smile curving her lips. "Maybe."

"Oh!" Lily sank back in her chair. "That's big. Isn't it?"

Happily, Beth nodded. "He's really big."

Lily stared at her, and then she started laughing, not stopping until Beth realized she had set herself up for an innuendo.

"That's not what I meant!" she protested, feeling the blood shoot back hot into her face. But even she could hear how weak her protest sounded—maybe because she was such a bad liar. Catching herself, she started laughing as well, waving her hand in the air as if she could shoo the entire exchange away.

"Good for you!" Lily said and lifted her cup to cheer.

"I'd have to agree," Beth admitted, keen to get off the subject.

"So what happens now?" Lily asked.

"Now we marry." Beth shook her head at Lily, letting her know she wasn't being serious. "I really don't know, honey. We'll see."

"Good luck." Lily smiled, and Beth could see she was being sincere. "He's a great guy, and you two are cute together."

"What about you?" Beth was done talking about herself. "How was your night out?

"Great! It was a real girls' night out, and we needed it. At least, I did." Lily picked up her fork, letting it hover over her plate of breakfast foods before choosing the fluffy soufflé pancake with the home-made raspberry sauce. "What was that text you just got?"

"It was the real estate agent." Beth cleared her throat. "Apparently, we have an offer. Over the asking price, but they want to move in quickly. The house is practically sold."

"Whoa." Lily stopped chewing. "That was fast! How are you feeling?"

"I feel...weird." Beth cut a piece of her Swiss quiche but didn't try it. "Sad, of course. Most of my life's past is tied up with that house. But also...happy."

"What makes you happy? The money?" Lily dipped her apricot croissant into her coffee.

"Don't dip, honey. It isn't good manners."

"But it tastes better." Unrepentant, Lily slurped up the soggy corner. "Ah! Delicious."

Beth smiled, moving the coffee cup away. "Of course the money is nice. But I'm happy because..." She paused for a moment. "It's a new beginning," she finally said, realizing the truth of it. She gazed thoughtfully at the vineyards, noting the golden light filtering through the leaves.

"Because why?" Lily set down her croissant, waiting for Beth to finish the sentence.

"Because I clung to that house for so long, convinced it was the last piece of Ben I had left—the last remnant of a life that I thought defined me. But now, I see it wasn't the house that mattered. It's the love I gave, the memories, the people who have come into my life. What I truly have isn't a past I'm trying to hold on to—it's a future, waiting to be filled with new memories and new love."

"I think that's amazing, Beth. You deserve a fresh start."

Beth smiled, grateful for her sweet companion. "Thank you, honey. The same goes for you, by the way. I'm sure your mother wanted nothing more than a bright future for you."

Lily nodded, pulling her coffee back toward her. "Do you think Ben wanted a new beginning for you?"

"Yes." Beth blinked back sudden tears, the thought of Ben always bittersweet. On his last night, he held her hand, whispering that he wanted to live, be with her, stay in his beautiful house. "He'd want me to be happy," she said, releasing the sadness from her heart and sending it into the golden hills and the sapphire sky, allowing the monarchs in the milkweed, the bees in the vines, the field larks trilling their morning songs, and the distant rumble of the ocean help carry her burden. "He'd want me to find love again." She smiled, her voice catching. "And he would have liked Mateo."

Lily nodded, but her expression shifted as the conversation drifted toward the thing neither of them had really touched yet. She took a slow breath, setting her cup down with more care than necessary. "Speaking of Ben... We haven't really talked about everything we found out." She paused, her hands fidgeting slightly. "You know...about him being my father."

Beth's throat clenched, the shock of the revelation still fresh in her mind. "I know," Beth said softly. "It's...a lot. I can't imagine how you're feeling, sweetheart. You were okay at first, but sometimes it takes time to sink in."

Lily bit her lip and shrugged, but her eyes were shiny too. "Honestly, I don't even know how I'm feeling. Angry, maybe, that Mom didn't let him know. Confused, sad...but also relieved." She exhaled. "Like, finally, I know who I am."

Beth reached across the table, taking Lily's hand in hers. "I'm pretty sure you've always known who you are, Lily. This doesn't change that."

Lily smiled faintly. "It kind of does, though. I mean, I grew up thinking my dad was some random deadbeat guy. Now, I find out it was Ben. Your Ben. The man you loved and a man who probably would've liked to know I exist."

"I wish I could change that, honey," Beth said, squeezing her hand. "I wish Ben had known. He would've loved you."

Tears welled up in Lily's eyes. "I just... It's weird, isn't it? That he never knew me, and now he's gone. I'll never get to know him, but...I'm here with you. And you knew him better than anyone."

Beth's chest tightened, her emotions tangled. There was guilt, surprisingly, that she got to know Lily when Ben couldn't. And sadness that she and Ben hadn't been able to have kids. There was a real dash of aggravation that in all their years together, he'd never once mentioned Maggie when she'd loved him so much.

But, once all these layers had been peeled back, Beth found that more than anything, she felt gratitude. Gratitude to have Lily, this sweet, bright young woman, in her life. "I agree, it is weird. But it's also right, in a way. I'm so glad you knocked on the door back then."

Lily rubbed her cheek with her wrist to wipe away a tear and nodded. "You're right. I'm really glad about that too. I'm real glad I have you, Beth."

For a moment, they sat in silence, hands clasped, their feelings hovering between them.

"Whatever this is—it isn't perfect and it isn't easy, but it's ours." Beth smiled. "I'm glad we have something that belongs to the two of us."

Lily smiled back. "I'm actually really glad you got Grandma's house. I would've had to sell it for the taxes, but you'll keep it in the family." She tilted her head, the teasing light from earlier returning to her pretty eyes. "I mean, sort of."

"We definitely are sort of family." The words warmed Beth's heart.

"Listen, if someone asks, just say it's complicated." A small giggle escaped Lily.

"Right." Beth exhaled, feeling lighter. It would take both of them time to come to peace with Ben's and

Maggie's decisions. But those decisions were part of the past, while Beth and Lily lived in the present, happily sitting together in a beautiful spot, eating pancakes and enjoying the warm sun, the sweet air, and most of all, each other's company. She made a gesture indicating it was time for them to move on. "So, what do you say? Shall we toast to fresh starts? To life and whatever's next?"

"Life, what's next, and, um, love. Definitely let's add love too." Lily grinned, raising her cup. "To new beginnings," she agreed, her voice warm with affection. "Cheers, coffee!"

Beth clinked her cup against Lily's, her heart swelling with pride at having this new sort-of daughter, who was surely the most generous, loving, kind, beautiful young woman to stumble into any sort-of mother's life. "To new beginnings," she echoed, grinning back at Lily.

Lily drank and then popped the last crisp rasher of bacon into her mouth. "Wasn't Hannah looking for a place to have that fundraiser meeting for the bookstore? What about here?"

Beth let her gaze wander over the luscious grapes below the terrace. "Maybe," she said. "I hear there's dancing at night."

"Bring Mateo," Lily said and giggled again.

"That's enough out of you, young lady." Beth tried to sound stern but didn't manage. "I'll suggest it to Hannah."

"Don't cut me out. I want to come for a last yahoo," Lily said.

"What do you mean, a last yahoo?" Alarmed, Beth looked up.

"I have a job and a shop and all that." Lily looked up, the giggling light in her eyes gone as quickly as it had come. "I really do need to go back to Maine."

CHAPTER 25

The sun was beginning to set over the hills, casting a warm, amber glow over the roofed terrace of the winery. The neat rows of grapevines stretched into the distance, their lobed leaves rustling in the evening breeze as laughter and the clinking of glasses filled the air.

The long table was laden with platters of antipasti, fresh bread, and bowls of salads. The rich scent of rosemary, garlic, and olive oil wafted up from the grilled vegetables, and the sound of corks popping open bottles of the winery's finest announced the start of a perfect evening.

Jenny and Jon, the vineyard owners, wandered arm in arm among their guests, stopping by Beth's table to discuss their catering services, only leaving when the band arrived to set up their instruments.

Hannah, sitting with Alex at the head of the table, looked radiant in a new red dress, her curls bouncing and her eyes sparkling as she raised her glass. "To a fabulous fundraiser for the bookshop! We're going to bring our little community together, and we're going to raise enough money to keep our little bookstore going for another season."

Alex clinked his glass with those he could reach, then rested his hand on Hannah's, smiling. "This is going to be one for the books—literally."

"Oh, funny, Alex. Just wait and see. It will be one for the books."

"That's what I said," he protested while Hannah, shaking her head at the pun, leaned in to kiss his cheek.

Sitting across from them, Beth smiled at their easy affection. They'd had to walk a rocky road to find each other, but now something had noticeably changed between them. Beth thought that, maybe, it meant the two were leaving the puppy love stage, delving into something deeper.

Her gaze drifted to Mateo, who was sitting beside her, leaning back in his chair with a contented expression. He was meeting her friends properly for the first time, but if he was nervous, it sure didn't show. "So, you're the one behind this?" Mateo asked, nodding at Hannah with an appreciative smile. "I'm impressed. I can't think of a better way to bring people together than books and wine."

"Well," Hannah said, her face lighting up even more, "it helps that everyone in this town loves both!"

"Where do you want to do it, Hannah?" Beth asked. She'd not heard the final word. "Here? Or in the store?"

"Actually, I was hoping to do it on the beach. We could set up reading blankets with lots of pillows, a bar for food and drinks, and a big book exchange table."

"I like the sound of that," Mateo said, immediately warming to the idea. "We don't have nearly enough community events."

"Exactly," Hannah agreed. "And we need everyone's help. Even Alex is getting in on the planning."

"I wouldn't dare say no," Alex teased, his starry eyes glinting. "Besides, who can resist a beach full of books?"

"Nobody." Mateo sipped from his glass in agreement. "I can set up a booth—I used to sell food at the farmers market."

Beth sat up. She'd spent most of the day in the old house, cleaning out the garage and wondering what she should do with twenty years' worth of Christmas lights. "I have a ton of light chains for the beach," she said eagerly.

"We can run a cord from the bookstore across the street and put lights everywhere." Across the table, Sara sat beside her husband, Andy, who was swirling his wine round and round in the expensive crystal glass as if it were a fiddle toy.

"No way you're allowed to run an extension cord across the street, Sara. Forget it," Andy said without looking up. A bit of his wine spilled, and he pushed the linen napkin into the puddle without stopping the swirling of his wine.

"It's not a busy street. I'm sure we can talk to—" Sara shot him a pleading look, clearly embarrassed by his behavior. "Andy, why don't you try some of the grilled vegetables? They're incredible."

"No," Andy muttered, not bothering to meet her eyes. "Vegetables are not my kind of thing; seems like you should know that by now. Quit nagging, please."

Mateo's gaze flickered to Andy, assessing him with a sharp glance. He leaned in slightly, his voice low as he said, "You know, Andy, trying something new now and then can surprise you. I wasn't sure I'd enjoy myself tonight, but now? I wouldn't want to be anywhere else."

"Grilled vegetables aren't exactly new to me, Matt. Not sure how you figure they can surprise me. But I guess you're a cook. Have to keep your hopes up when it comes to people eating your vegetables, eh?"

Mateo leaned back, his eyes thoughtful. "I do keep my hopes up," he agreed. "That's another thing you could try sometime."

Andy glanced at him, his frown deepening. He didn't reply, but at least he finally stopped swirling his wine and set down the glass.

Sara looked mortified, and Beth felt a tug of sympathy for her friend, who was clearly struggling with her husband's attitude. Andy had been weighing Sara down for years, and from the little Sara had shared with her book club friends, it was getting worse, not better. Sara had decided to fix the marriage, but it didn't seem to be working.

Lightly tapping Sara's shin with her foot below the table to get her attention, Beth smiled. "Sara, if you have time this Friday, I'd love some help testing the lights before I bring them to the beach. I'm sure some of them need new fuses or bulbs. Or are you still busy with that new case at work?"

Sara forced a smile, gratefully accepting the distraction. "I'll come out to the house to help. The case is all wrapped up. You're right; it was a lot. But worth it."

Mateo picked up a bottle, grinning as he refilled Alex's empty glass. "So you run a bookstore—are you the quiet, thoughtful type?"

Alex grinned back. "More like I need a job where no one's shooting at me."

"You're joking."

"Not as much as I wish he was," Hannah threw in, pointing at the bulge of Alex's bandage under his button-up shirt.

Following her gaze, Mateo raised an eyebrow. "Books and food—they're both about survival, eh? Just different kinds."

Alex nodded. "Yeah, one keeps you alive, the other keeps you sane. I'm a fan of both."

"Amen, my friend." Mateo raised his glass to that. "So do you read your books, or are you just hiding behind them?"

"I read," Alex said and finally had to laugh. "I read a lot. It's my one redeeming quality. How about yourself?"

"I do when I have time. It's an escape," Mateo said. "Cooking is my life, but books...they're a getaway from my life. I actually worked in a little bookstore for a few months when I was a student."

"Where?" Interested, Alex leaned forward. Their talk about books mixed with the general hum of chatter and the first notes of soft jazz music from the band. But when Mateo turned to Andy, trying to draw him in, the attempt fell flat.

"Not much of a reader?" Mateo asked good-naturedly, but Andy just shrugged.

"Real literature is so rare; it's not even worth my time looking for it. And I really don't need to read a book where I can predict the whole plot on page two. I mean, surprise me—but who can manage that anymore, right? Name one dang author with the chops."

"Plots are like vegetables and hope, Andy," Alex threw in. "Can't tell without trying them."

"Yeah, well, I don't like vegetables. Sue me."

Hannah glanced at Beth, signaling her exasperation with Andy. "Well, speaking of books, I'm thinking we could have a little auction, maybe have some signed editions or local authors give readings."

"That sounds great," Sara murmured. "Andy, what are you—where are you going?"

Her husband rose, setting his napkin on the table. "I think I'll leave. Someone has to take care of the kids after all, and Sara is hardly ever at home. Can't leave 'em alone all evening."

"The kids are staying at their friends', Andy. Please don't leave." Usually so vivacious, Sara was frozen with embarrassment. But Andy had already clapped a hand on Alex's shoulder as if the two of them were buddies, in it together, and left without looking back.

Beth tried to pull her attention back to the main topic. "I like the auction idea," she said, smiling support at Sara. "What about if kids come?"

Sara cleared her throat twice before speaking. "We could have a little section for them—maybe set up special blankets with picture books and sand toys, so families can enjoy the day too."

"I think I still have an ice cream cart somewhere," Mateo said. "If it still works, I'll look up some of my old recipes and whip up a few batches."

"Ice cream, sand, water, kids, and books?" Alex sounded a little doubtful. "Are we sure about this?"

"What kind of man asks that? Don't you like kids?" Mateo grinned at him.

Alex spread his hands in defense. "I do! I like kids. I'm just asking."

"I think it sounds fantastic!" Hannah said. "Let me know about the ice cream cart, Mateo. I've already got a few people lined up who could help watch kids. It's going to be perfect."

Just then, a teen server appeared with trays of steaming dishes—pasta tossed with fresh basil and tomatoes, tender lamb with rosemary, and a delicate lemon risotto that filled the air with its citrusy fragrance. The whole table quieted for a moment as everyone admired the feast before them.

Beth glanced over at Mateo, who was watching her with a smile. She felt a wave of emotion wash over her—something deep and comforting.

A few weeks ago, the book club meetings had been her only lifeline to friends and community. Now, she was surrounded by good people, good food, and new beginnings. She wasn't alone. Not anymore. She felt herself slipping into the joy of the evening, the laughter of her friends filling the air as they ate.

She looked over at Mateo again, her heart swelling at the thought of what lay ahead for them. He leaned closer, his voice low and full of affection. "You okay, Bella?"

She nodded. "I'm more than okay."

"Good. Forgive me," he murmured in her ear when he kissed her cheek. "Have the tiramisu and think of me."

Forgive what? Beth was going to ask when the band changed from one melody to another, and he stood.

"Are you done?" He smiled at Sara.

She looked up. Hardly having touched her food, she set down her silverware, looking grateful that she could stop pretending. "I am. It was delicious."

"Would you like to dance?" He held out a hand, and after a moment of surprise, Sara took it and let him help her stand.

"Actually, I would like to dance," she said, glancing for permission at Beth.

Smiling, Beth winked at her friend. There was nothing to make a hurting heart feel better than dancing on a warm, starry night. Even if poor Sara was married to a man forever stuck in his terrible twos.

"How about dessert, ladies?" Alex looked from Beth to Hannah, lifting the bottle to refill their glasses. "I hear it's yummy."

"Yes, please." Beth smiled, moving her chair to be closer to the couple. "I'll have the tiramisu."

CHAPTER 26

The sun had met the sea in a long, lingering kiss and sunk, besotted, into her blue arms while a silver moon rose to watch over lovers and dancers. Night was spreading her sparkling veil over the landscape, coloring the hills lavender and plum, and cicadas and fireflies celebrated the arrival of her protection. Happy, Beth leaned against a wooden post, watching Mateo from across the space, his face illuminated by the twinkling lights strung below the roof of the terrace. Laughter and music filled the air; she couldn't hear what he was saying, but he was speaking to Alex and Jon. Likely, they were discussing the fundraiser event.

The men shared an easy grin, and she smiled at the sight. The fundraiser was a brilliant idea, and Beth was convinced the entire town would show up, buzzing with support—especially if Mateo was part of it. There were few people in the area he didn't know since the community faithfully patronized its precious handful of restaurants.

There was something so effortlessly charming about the evening—the camaraderie, the wine, the laughter—that Beth felt herself slipping into it, letting go of the moving chaos that had been her life just hours before. Despite the hired crew, there was so much to do. With Lily's help, she had spent most of the week clearing out the sold house, sorting through the last boxes of memories, and preparing for the move into the cottage. It had been emotionally taxing, no doubt about it. But her new life had too much promise to be overwhelmed by memories. She couldn't wait to start it fully.

"Beth." Mateo's voice, rich and low, pulled her out of her thoughts. He was walking toward her, his gaze intent as he closed the distance between them. The smile on his lips made her heart skip. "You disappeared on me. What are you doing over here all alone?"

She shrugged lightly, her smile deepening at the sight of him. "Just taking it all in. It's a beautiful night, isn't it?"

"Sure." Mateo's eyes searched hers in that way of reading her so easily. He reached out and took her hand, his thumb brushing against her knuckles. "You've had a lot on your plate lately."

Beth exhaled. Did she look frazzled? She was feeling rather pretty actually, wearing the new summer dress Lily had promised flattered her figure. "Literally or figuratively?"

He shook his head, chuckling at the little joke, but not letting himself be sidetracked. "It's a lot, packing up the last twenty years to move. You're downsizing, getting rid of so many things that have memories attached. Does it make you sad?"

Beth looked down at their hands. It really was hard. All the photo albums, the trinkets, the books...so, so many books. Ben's books. She couldn't think too much, sorting through it, training her thoughts firmly on the future. "I get to keep the memories, and I'll have to let go of the material things sooner or later. I hope someone else can make new memories with them."

"Yeah?"

She sighed, admitting, "Sometimes, I take a photo before putting something in a donation box."

"I like that you get to keep the memories," he said gently. "It's what's in the heart and the mind that counts."

"I agree." She nodded. "The move is going well, and you and I..." She trailed off, not quite able to articulate the emotions rising inside her. If there was an area of overwhelm in her life, it was this flood of new happiness, new experiences, and thoughts that came with dating Mateo.

He gave her hand a soft squeeze. "You and I are good," he said, his voice a steady anchor. "Listen, I've been meaning to tell you something. But I don't want it to worry you."

Never in the history of womanhood had those words had the intended effect... Beth bit her lip, glancing up at her handsome man. Already, she had lain awake some nights, wondering if this second chance at love was too good to be true. Straightening her back, she braced herself. "What's that, Mateo?"

"Do you remember when I mentioned my family? We are very close."

"We talked about your parents, who retired in Rome."

He nodded. "But I also have cousins and siblings—quite a lot of them, really."

"I didn't know." She tilted her head, surprised he'd not talked about them. She hadn't thought to ask after anyone but the mother, who loved her friends and the fountains of Rome, and the father, who was, Mateo claimed, a much better chef than himself.

"We have so much to talk about; it never came up before." He smiled, his expression warm. "But now, everyone's coming for a visit."

Her heart fluttered again, this time in a different way. "A visit," she repeated. "A family reunion."

"We have a lot of them. It's a big, social family." Mateo's eyes danced with a smile, but there was a seriousness in his tone too. "They want to meet you, Beth. They're excited to get to know you."

"You told them about me?" Beth felt her breath catch. Of course, she'd dragged him along tonight, eager for him to meet her sisters of the heart and her found family. But...real family? What could he possibly have told them about her? They'd only dated for such a short time. "Your family... I'm just—are you sure?"

"Sure? Sure about what? My feelings for you?" He stepped closer, wrapping his arms around her waist, pulling her into him. The warmth of his body and the steadiness of his touch made everything easy as she relaxed into him.

"You know what I mean," she whispered. "Everything is so recent."

"Maybe. But you're everything I've wanted to introduce them to," he murmured against her hair, his lips brushing her ear. "Besides, it's not just about them."

Beth pulled back slightly to see his face. "What do you mean?"

"I mean..." Mateo's eyes darkened, his hands tightening gently on her waist. "Do you want to meet them? They're not just my family. If you want them, they can be yours too."

"Mine?"

He nodded, his eyes searching hers. "It's a big, loud, happy family. Most of the time, it's great. Sometimes, it can be...well." He chuckled at the thought of past drama. "But it doesn't matter. It's family."

"Mateo—do we know each other well enough for this?" The words grated in her throat, sounding wrong and thorny. Because she wanted Mateo. She wanted Mateo with every fiber of her being. But wasn't it supposed to take a long time to get to this point? Wasn't it supposed to be harder to finally get to the point of whispering that magical word family in each other's ears?

"I think so," he said simply. "I'm almost fifty, Beth. All my life, I've searched. And I finally found you. I know what I want."

"Mateo," she said weakly, meeting his gaze. She also knew, knew from the first time she walked into his restaurant.

"What is it?" He took a step back, giving her space.

"Nothing." The opening between them felt terrible—full of air, vacuum, night. She wanted him to come back, to close it again, to want her enough to tolerate her doubt.

"This life, my future... I want it with you," he said softly, wiping a strand of hair from her face. "I want to give you everything—myself, my work, my family. It may not always be easy; life isn't. But I'm not afraid. If you want it too, you can't be afraid either, Beth. If you don't want it, tell me. But don't hide from it."

Beth stared at him, her heart thudding in her chest as the sincerity in his eyes and voice sank in. A shared future. A family. He was offering her his heart, his time, his trust—everything.

This wasn't just about starting to date again or selling a house and moving. It wasn't even about closing one chapter and opening another. It was about choosing a whole new book, opening herself to a life so much bigger than she'd imagined possible for herself. With Mateo. With a family. With everything that came with that. And the truth was...she did want it. She wanted it all. The mess, the chaos, the love. The family she'd always been missing, the warmth of belonging, not just with Mateo, but with the people who loved him too.

"Will they like me?" she asked softly, feeling more like her insecure twenty-year-old self rather than her middle-aged self. "What if they don't like me?"

A smile tugged at the corner of his lip. "I will slap them with gloves and polish my pistols if they don't," he murmured. "Of course they'll like you. They'll adore you."

"I want it," she said, surprising even herself with the strength in her voice. "I want your family, Mateo. I want you. I want everything you bring into my life."

He smiled, his eyes closing for a moment as if he'd been waiting to hear those words and now savored them, drawing them down to the core of his being. "Then it's yours, Beth," he said when he opened them again. "All of it. And you"—he pulled her closer, closing that unbearable space between them—"you are mine." He smiled, his lips lightly brushing over hers. "You were mine a long time ago," he murmured. "I've waited for you to come to town, to the restaurant. And you finally did come, with your Venetian eyes and your Florentine figure, your sweet, sad thoughts and your angel voice." He exhaled, his breath mingling with hers. "That's how I felt when I saw you sitting at the table by the window—as if the marble statue of an angel had come to life and smiled at me, letting me know I was yours." He drew a breath. "I wanted to take your hand. I wanted to kiss the tips of your fingers, the warm center of your palm, make you feel loved as you should be loved."

Beth felt a rush of warmth spread through her, the last of her nerves melting as she leaned into him. "Why didn't you? I thought you were the most attractive man I ever met." She looked up. "I still do."

"You wouldn't have liked me to say much more than I did." His smile reached his eyes. "I even had to send another server to your table to control myself."

Beth remembered her disappointment at having another server come to her table only too well...but maybe Mateo was right. Maybe she'd still been too firmly rooted in her old life to let herself flirt with him. But that was over. "Kiss me now," she whispered, tilting her head back.

Mateo lowered his head and kissed her, soft and sure. The music swelled around them, stars blinked to life, and something clicked into place for them.

Beth smiled against his lips, sinking into his arms, knowing that his love, his generosity, and his commitment were already changing her into someone sweeter, kinder, someone ready to both give and receive all the love, hope, and happiness of a beautiful life.

"I love you, Beth." His voice was as soft as the dark-blue velvet of the night sky. It was the first time he'd said the words, but they sounded like they came from the deepest part of his being.

"I love you too, Mateo," she said softly, knowing it was true, knowing she was giving herself, her heart and soul and body, fully to him.

As if he sensed she was dropping her last defenses, he drew a sharp breath, his arms tightening protectively around her. She put her hands on his chest, feeling his heart beat steady and strong. "Take good care of me," she whispered.

"You are my life now," he said, lifting her hands to his mouth to kiss first them, then her lips. "Do you want to go home?"

"Why?" She smiled. "Do you want me to get the house ready for your big, loud family?"

He pulled away, laughter in his eyes. "They do arrive in two days," he admitted. "But cleaning is not exactly at the top of my list right now."

"You have a whole list?" She giggled.

He slipped her arm into his, holding it tight, and she felt him move, guiding her off the dance floor. "Let's go to my place. I'll show you my list," he murmured.

"Yes, I'd like to check a few things." She giggled, and together, they walked out into the sweet, cooling night.

CHAPTER 27

H enry!" Lily waved as the rusty, old yellow pickup truck with the peeling hippie stickers came to a creaking stop in the cottage's driveway. In the back, she spotted her chair. It was secured with a net of bungee cords, the old fabric looking even more faded in the bright sun than it had in the shop window of the island's antique store. "Hi! Welcome!" she called.

The old shop owner leaned out the open window and grinned. "Hi, kid," he said, leaning his elbow on the window. "How are you?"

"Good." Lily came to open the door for him. When she saw how heavy he really was, she held out a hand to help him. "What's up?"

He accepted her help, huffing and puffing with the effort of climbing out. "Get my cane, will you, sweetie? It's on the...over there." Too hard of breath to explain more, he pointed over his shoulder. "I'm old and fat, or I'd get it myself."

"Sure." A little worried about the old man's condition, Lily hurried around the truck, her strappy leather sandals twirling up the warm dust on the ground. She snatched the cane—not a proper one, but a thick wooden staff, like that of a medieval magician—and brought it to him. "Why don't you come in?" She took his free hand to support him.

"If you're sure," he groaned. "Don't mean to be a bother."

"No bother," she assured him. "We've been waiting for you. Beth made little Greek yogurt treats she found on a website about diabetes diets."

Henry stopped in the shade of the cottage to rest. "She has diabetes too?"

"No." Lily smiled. "She looked it up especially for you, Henry. By the way, she's the girl Ben Thompson married after he and my mother broke up. So no more talk about consolation prizes, all right? They had a very happy marriage."

"Dang." He stroked his beard, a stumped expression on his face. "Should I apologize?"

"I think maybe let's just not talk about it again," Lily said delicately. "Ben passed away a few years ago, and she's just getting over it. Best not to stir up the deep, dark past."

"It doesn't bother you, hmm?" Despite the wrinkles and the white beard, Henry's eyes were those of a young man when he searched her face.

"No. It doesn't," she said firmly. "Ben didn't know about me and never came looking for us. He was a good man and a good husband to Beth. But I don't all of a sudden have strong feelings about him just because I share half his genes."

"All righty then." The watchful eyes disappeared again behind heavy lids. "Sounds like you and Maggie didn't miss out."

"I don't know about Mom. I had dreams about who he was, and my dreams sure were better than a high school date who quickly moved on. But you know something else? Because of my father, I now have a solid connection to Beth. That, I like very much. I take it as his legacy to me. Unexpected family, when I thought I had no one left."

"Ah." He nodded. "Yes, that's good. Well, I won't mention him. No point in stirring an empty pot, anyway."

"Thanks." She smiled. "Shall we have another go at getting inside?"

"I wish I wasn't so fat," he said and leaned on his cane to take a step. "It makes everything so hard. If I don't lose my gut, the diabetes is going to kill me, Dr. Summers said. He's a nice kind of guy, but he doesn't mince words. Looked me deep in the eyes too."

Lily let him huff over the threshold before following him inside. "Did Dr. Summers say what to do about it?" She raised her eyebrows.

He wheezed a chuckle. "Sure did. His wife, Hazel—she's got a little wedding dress store not so far from my shop and she brings me lunch sometimes. She gave me a bunch of brochures and websites." He looked around the living room, a guilty expression on his face. "I never eat the salads she brings me. Rabbit food, I think... My Annelise used to spoil me with cream sauces and hearty stews. She was from Austria, you know. Such good cooking."

"Yes, well, I doubt your Annelise would give you cream sauces if the doctor says to eat salad," Lily said briskly. "I'm sure she loved you too much to want you to have diabetes."

Henry narrowed his eyes. "You do remind me of your mother."

The door in the kitchen creaked open, and a moment later, Beth came around the corner. "Henry! Lily! I thought we'd sit outside in the garden."

Lily raised her eyebrows to signal *I'm trying* while Henry held out his hand. "I hear you made me yogurt treats."

"I did indeed." Smiling, Beth shook. "Come on through—take your time and watch the step. I'll get us iced tea. I hope unsweetened is okay."

Henry shuffled on, a little quicker now that they were in the cool, even-floored house. "I've never had a yogurt treat."

"They are very good," Mateo's deep voice came from the kitchen, and then he appeared, taking off his apron. "Henry, my friend! You never come to my restaurant anymore!"

"I'd like to," Henry said, his face lightening up. "I dream of your carbonara at night. But that's what got me in trouble in the first place, young man."

"All my fault, eh?" Laughing, Mateo took Henry's arm while clapping a hand on his shoulder. "Go running with me, old man. Up and down the beach, just you and me and the fresh air. Tomorrow at dawn."

Henry wheezed another laugh as he went onto the patio and heavily sank into a chair. "I can't tomorrow at dawn. Or dusk. But thanks for offering." Wiping the sweat off his forehead, he looked around the rambling garden, the swaying grasses and flowers, curiosity in his gaze. "So this is where Maggie lived, huh? I feel like I know it—though I've never been. My wife dropped off Maggie a few times when she helped out and told me about it. I always thought it would be pretty."

Ice cubes clinked as Beth set the glass pitcher with peach tea on the table and took a seat. "Well, now you have to come visit me all the time," she said cheerfully while Lily rose to pour the tea. "I just moved into town and would love to make more friends."

"I can't..." Shaking his head, Henry interrupted himself. "I'll try," he said and lifted his glass. "I could use new friends too."

Mateo, joining them with a bowl of frozen yogurt treats, frowned. "You are lonely, Henry?"

"It's so hard to get around." Henry patted his belly. "My joints are at war with my stomach. And who comes into a dusty antique store with a fat old man? I can't reach the corners I have to dust."

"I'm putting you on a diet," Mateo declared. "We'll take care of you. Here. Try this." He set the bowl down.

He eyed it. "How does it taste?"

"Ah! If I make it, you don't ask. You put it in your mouth and praise me." Mateo's charming smile belied the bossy tone. "But if you need to know, they are berries, coated in a layer of dark chocolate so thin my thoughts can melt it. Dipped in yogurt, and frozen." He leaned forward. "Enjoy the chocolate—thin or not, there won't be any more of it. I didn't know how fat you really were. You always sit behind that counter, hiding it," he murmured.

"Eh." Looking unconvinced, Henry popped a treat in his mouth and chewed. "Oh. Mmm. Okay. Okay." He took another one.

Mateo leaned back with a satisfied expression on his face and crossed his arms. "You brought the chair?"

"It's in the back of the truck. I had a heck of a time getting it up there." Henry sighed and leaned back. "Now I want to eat them all. I can't do things by half, at least not when it comes to food. Sometimes, I think I should just stop eating for a year. What do you think, chef?"

"I think you should eat more vegetables," Mateo declared and got up. "I'll go get the chair."

"Thank you," Lily and Beth said in unison, and Henry chuckled.

"So you and Mateo, huh?" He turned to Beth after Mateo left. "He's a good man," Henry said thoughtfully. "I always wondered why he wasn't married ten times over."

"I was waiting for her," Mateo called from the kitchen. "That's why, Henry. She's my angel, and you only get one."

Henry nodded. "I found my angel too," he said after a moment. "It was bliss. I miss my Annelise every day; there never was another woman for me."

"I know," Beth said gently, putting a hand on Henry's arm. "I know. But you don't have to be alone, Henry. We're here."

"What's the word for a male angel?" Lily sipped her tea.

"I think it's the same." Henry smiled. "Looking for yours?"

Lily grimaced and nodded. After her last breakup, she'd figured she came after Mom, footloose and fancy-free. She'd *not* figured that maybe, Mom had been helplessly in love her whole life, her heart lost to a man who never called, never visited, never looked back enough to send a postcard.

"Lily?" Beth looked at her with concern in her eyes.

"Yes? Yes!" Lily pulled herself together, smiling and sitting up straight. Meeting dateable men was a real problem. She didn't like the thought of online dating apps, but maybe it was time to try them.

"Henry would like the recipe for your cucumber salad."

"My what? Oh. Yes, of course. It's on my phone. If you give me your number, I'll text it to you."

"Text—yeah, I don't really know how to..." Henry fumbled with his phone, his other hand searching the top of his head for reading glasses.

"It's okay," Lily said quickly. "I can write it down for you—or even better, I'll make it for you. I'll just have to get peppers and cucumbers. Maybe I can get your groceries while I'm at it?" She remembered how hard it was for him to get around. Surely, there was a better course of exercise than shopping or running at dawn to get Henry moving.

"I know," Beth said suddenly. "Henry, do you like to garden?"

"I used to have a great garden. A great garden. But when I lost my Annelise, I stopped going out there."

Lily leaned forward. "Now that I have the chair, I'll need to weed my way to the garden shed; the path is completely overgrown. Maybe you'd like to help me?"

"I don't know if I can..." Still, the old man's gaze wandered to the wild corner of the property Lily indicated, an interested light in his eyes.

"You can clip the flowers," Lily promised. "I'll do the heavy weeding. It's nicer exercise than going grocery shopping, and you won't have to get up at dawn either. It works out."

"I mean..." He looked at Beth. "If it's not too much for me to come over now and then?"

"I'd love to have you anytime, Henry," she declared, looking delighted. "And since Mateo's carbonara got you in trouble, I'm sure he'll have no problem helping you with a healthy meal plan too." She leaned forward, smiling. "Listen, we're having a fundraiser at the beach tomorrow afternoon, to benefit the local bookstore. It would be nice if you could come."

His beard twitched as he smiled back. "Going places two days in a row? It'll be a whole new me."

Lily reached out to pat his arm. "Give Beth and Mateo half a year. You'll be slim and trim in no time, I'm sure."

"Beth and Mateo?" He turned to her. "And where are you going to be, little Lily?"

Beth looked up as well. "Yes, what are your plans, honey? You know you'll always have a home here."

Lily exhaled, letting her gaze wander past the blooming rhododendrons and flowering irises to the shimmering blue sea. "I have to leave soon," she said, hearing the sadness in her voice. "Once I finish fixing the chair, I have to get back to Maine."

CHAPTER 28

G athering the skirt of the flowy halter-top dress she'd bought for the occasion, Hannah turned just in time to see the playful breeze flip another book open. It hardly mattered since there were a gazillion more fluttering book pages surrounding them, but she felt like she should at least try to control the situation.

Taking a tablecloth-weight shaped like a strawberry, she closed the book and set the heavy berry on top. Putting her hands on her hips, she rose to survey their handiwork. The warm, golden beach was covered with cheerful pillows and picnic blankets, each held down by books readers could browse and take home for a small donation. In between the sunny reading spots stood beautifully artistic wicker baskets, a loan from the local basket weaving club. They were filled with pretty flowers and stuffed to the brim with home-baked treats like crispy cheese straws, pistachio and orange-blossom biscotti, and spiced honey cakes.

Closer to the water sat a chest filled with donated sand toys and buckets for the kids. Toward the direction of the store, tables draped in fluttering linen displayed the more expensive books for sale. A retired printer from Maytown, a friend of Alex's dad, had unexpectedly donated bookmarks, journals, and pretty linen totes, all featuring the new bookstore logo Hannah had designed for the event's announcement poster.

Last but not least, the picture was completed by long, wooden benches, coolers of soft drinks, juice, and water, and boxes of wine and glasses from the winery. The winery's kitchen staff had generously pitched in, setting up a banquet table filled with cheeses, charcuterie, quiches, prosciutto-wrapped melon, and freshly baked herbed focaccia. All the delicious offerings were perfectly paired with the wines, ready for those who wanted a bite to enjoy alongside their drink.

Alex and Jon were busy setting up torches and poles with twinkle lights that Beth had insisted on donating to the effort from her overflowing Christmas funds.

Sara and Alli came over, carrying leftover flowers and books, to stand by Hannah. "Hey, look," Sara whispered excitedly. "Our first guests!"

"Where?" Alli asked, jiggling baby Tommy on her hip. "Oh! Oh, they're so young! Teen girls."

Hannah slid her sunglasses down. The teenagers, tan, skinny, hair flowing in the sea breeze like in a shampoo commercial, were giggling and laughing, making a beeline for a pink quilt made by the local quilting circle. None of them acknowledged any of the adults putting the finishing touches on the setting. Instead, they dropped their backpacks and plopped down on the quilt, facing the sea.

Hannah grinned, feeling the teens' exuberant energy drift along with their laughter as they teased each other. "Is this good? Or are we in trouble?"

"You can never tell with teenagers... What are they doing?" Beth had joined them, peering over their shoulders. "Oh. Look! They're really here for the books!"

Each girl had grabbed a book. At first, they tussled over the most popular one, but soon they stretched out on the blanket, never minding that their tan legs and pointy elbows kept bumping each other as they started to read.

"Well, well, well, what a pretty picture." Hannah pushed her glasses back up her nose. "If that's not good advertising, I don't know what is. Hey, look—there's a family. I think they're coming our way."

Soon, it became clear that the event needed no pretty advertisement. People started to stream onto the beach, happily claiming the comfy quilts and blankets, many adding their own. The area continuously and busily expanded, and it seemed that some people had even brought their own books along, either donating them at the table, where Alex set up an impromptu book swap, or simply reading them.

More and more food and drinks arrived as well, and then two local authors began to read. One of them was a children's author who had brought crayons and paper, keeping the kids in their swimsuits spellbound. The other writer was a rom-com writer, who made the teenage girls twitter and giggle and snort lemonade up their noses.

Hannah was busy selling books until darkness lowered herself over the beach like a soft, broody hen. Alli left with two new mysteries and a plate of foil-wrapped quiche and honey cake in her hands to put Tommy to bed. Beth and Sara plugged in the Christmas lights, ribbing each other mercilessly and doubling over with laughter. Hannah watched as their poles twinkled to life, the lights shimmering and dancing in the rising tide like the songs of mermaids.

"Happy with your work, babe?" Alex stepped up beside her, wrapping his arm around her waist and pulling her close. "Because you should be. I had no idea we had so many readers in the area."

Nodding, Hannah leaned into him. "I saw almost everyone in town, plus people visiting from the cove and the island. Jenny drove a group of her students over from Maytown, and Audrey even rented vans for her hotel guests. So yes—it went much better than I'd hoped for. I'm glad people brought so much food, or we'd have run out hours ago. I hope the donations match the enthusiasm."

She could feel him smile as he kissed the top of her head. "Enough to pay the mortgage half a year out."

"You don't have a mortgage, Alex." The little bookshop had been in his family for generations.

"Then maybe we'll go on a nice vacation. How do you feel about a week in Hawaii?"

"Alexander! Really." Playfully, she swatted his arm. "The money is for the bookstore! You can finally bring it up to speed."

"We can bring it up to speed, you mean." He kissed her again. "Listen—about that." He cleared his throat, and the earnest note tinting the sound suddenly made the blood run cold in her veins.

Shocked, she twirled around to look at him. "Alex? Don't tell me you have to leave again! Your gun wound has barely healed! You said you were going to stay, you said—I can't lose you, Alex, I really cannot."

He pulled her fully into his embrace. "Shh. I'm not going anywhere, Hannah. I was—that's not what I meant to say."

Weak with relief, she let herself sink into the safety of his wide, strong chest, allowing the steady beat of his heart to soothe her. "Promise?" She looked up into his starry eyes, scrutinizing them for the urge to protect her from bad news. "You won't sneak off? You'll be here tomorrow morning?"

"I promise. I'll be here. Tomorrow morning, every morning." His blue eyes were earnest when he took her hands in his. "Hannah—that's what I want to talk about."

"What do you mean?"

"We talked about my place, your place..." He smiled. "We never came to a decision, did we?"

"I know, and I'm sorry, I can—" Hannah stopped herself mid-breath and exhaled. She was panicking. "I think maybe...I don't really understand what you mean?"

"Yes, I know." He chuckled, running a hand through his hair. "Because I'm making a mess of saying it."

"I like having you stay at the cottage," Hannah said, almost shyly. "I'm sorry if back then, on the beach...if it sounded anything other than that. I really like waking up beside you. I like coming down when you're in the kitchen, making coffee. I adore it when you bake cinnamon buns and the house smells so good. I..."

He reached for her, running a thumb down her jaw. "You like it... Hannah, I don't know if like is good enough for me."

If she'd thought before that her blood was running cold, then it was positively freezing now. "What do you mean?" she whispered. "I love you. I love you, Alex. With everything I have."

"Do you?" His warm thumb, rough from setting up the community event all day, had reached her lower lip. "With everything you have?"

Mute, she nodded. "I thought...I thought everything was good. Last night—"

She felt his body tense with the memory as he glanced over her head. "Hush," he murmured. "There are children present. Last night was—" For a moment, he grappled for words. "Fantastic," he murmured finally. "Last night was out of this world. For me, anyway." He tucked his chin to see her eyes.

Far from reassured, the ice crystals in her blood welded into glaciers. No way could she stand the tension, the fear of him saying she wasn't enough, he needed more. "It was for me too," she whispered, taking his hand. "Let's go back there. No children, see?" She pulled him along, the soft, warm sand giving under her feet as she reached the edge of the water and stepped out of the soft glow of the twinkle lights, into the softly lapping water.

Here, there was only the silver light of the moon, the rushing of the waves, the silence of the stars. Music and laughter drifted over to them, but the sounds were quickly swallowed by the warm night.

"Hannah." Alex pulled his hand from hers. "Wait. Wait."

She twirled around. "Are you going to tell me that you're breaking up with me, Alex?"

Before she could regret letting the words slip past her lips, he caught her in his arms. "Are you crazy?" he murmured, his embrace warm and firm and protective. "I'm not breaking up with you, Hannah. I'm trying to propose to you."

The ice in her veins broke apart, melted by the hot blush rushing to her face. "You—what?"

"I'm—I was trying to—" Alex laughed, suddenly letting her go to step back. "Do you want to marry me, Hannah?"

"I just got divorced!" Hannah slapped a hand to her mouth, shocked. "Sorry! Alex, I'm sorry. I don't know why I said that."

"Well, I do," he said reasonably. "You did just get divorced. I was afraid that's how you felt. It's just...I love you. When I got shot, right the moment the bullet hit me—I don't know, Hannah. I'd sure have died a happier man if we'd been man and wife in the face of God." He exhaled. "Can't claim I'm the religious type. But if being married gets me a better chance of seeing you again up there, or down, or sideways..." He cleared his throat. "No matter how long the wait, Hannah. At least I would get to wait. I think—I think I need you to be mine hook, line and sinker, page and chapter, kiss and signature. In short..." He took a deep breath. "I want all of you. I'm done waiting to ask. Marry me. Please."

"I just got divorced, Alex." Hannah tasted the words. They tasted wrong, like hay when she expected to taste honey. Dry and brittle and bitter.

He groaned. "I'll wait. Hannah, I'll—"

"No." She put her hands on his chest, feeling his heart race. She'd never felt it beat so fast before. "No. I don't care about that, Alex. Because my marriage was over many years ago. Truly and honestly, it was dead; I just didn't know it. I was shaking its lifeless body, medicating it, dressing it up as if it was still alive, as if there was still a chance... I didn't know better. I didn't know the freedom I'd feel finally leaving that prison. I didn't know how light and airy I could feel if I cut loose a man who was, at best, not in love with me."

She stepped closer. The breeze played with her hair, a single curl reaching for Alex as if every part of her longed for him.

"Here's what else I didn't know," she whispered. "I didn't know how glorious it is to be loved by a good man. I didn't know how amazingly mind-blowing it is to feel your skin on mine, your hands, your body. I didn't know that all this time, all these years, I was desperate for you."

With a groan of longing, Alex lowered his head, pressing his lips on hers. "I have your ring, but I didn't bring it," he murmured when they surfaced again. "I wasn't going to do this tonight; I was going to take you out, forcing myself to wait another six months if I could stand it, get down on my knee, do it properly. But when I saw you standing there, so sweet and kind and strong all at the same time, the light shimmering on your dress and in your beautiful eyes... I adore you. I've always adored you. I will love you forever. I'd rather get shot at again than wait any longer. The wedding can wait if you want—but I need to know you are mine."

"I'm yours." Smiling, Hannah cradled his face in her hands. "I'm yours, hook, line and sinker," she promised. "I'm yours for every chapter, page, and word that is to come. I love you, Alex." She rose on her toes, kissing him softly, whispering against his lips. "I will love you forever."

CHAPTER 29

Henry tucked the gardening shears into the tiny gardening apron Beth had loaned him. The apron barely fit around his vast belly, but it saved him enough bending and searching and fetching that, to Lily's undisguised delight, he insisted on wearing it when clipping the roses into shape. Now, too, as she walked to meet him by the little garden shed that they had turned into her studio, she thought how funny and cute it made the old man look. Like a funny, dear, fat Santa Claus.

"Hey," she said and slipped her arm under his. "How are you? Not getting too hot?"

"Still standing." From a second pocket, Henry pulled a blue bandanna with a faded paisley pattern, then he took off his ancient straw hat and wiped his forehead. "Looks nice," he said, scrutinizing the shed. "I left the roses growing around the window so they'll frame your view." He nodded, content, and stuffed the bandanna back. "I clipped them pretty good, if I say so myself."

"You sure did." Lily smiled. She'd never get tired of his barely disguised joy at having found a new hobby—and new people who cared. Slowly, his life had shrunk to the store and doctor visits after he lost his wife, and for years, he'd not been able to get himself to care. But once the worst of the grief softened, fraying around edges that let a little bit of hope and happiness back in, he'd gotten lonely. By then, most of his friends were gone, and few people had an interest in coming to his dusty store. Plus, he'd found himself an involuntary prisoner of his health.

Now, he'd come out to the beach house a couple of times, ready to help Lily clear out the shed. She knew she tethered him to his past and the people he missed so much. And for her, it was a little bit like finally having the jolly old grandpa she'd never had.

The easy gardening and the newfound company did him good. He looked better, healthier. When he visited, Mateo had healthy, nourishing meals ready to take back home, enough to get him through until the next visit. When he found out that Henry had no freezer, he and Alex installed one in his kitchen. Meanwhile, Lily, Beth, Sara, and Hannah folded up their sleeves, donned sturdy gloves, and gave his living quarters a thorough, much-needed, top-to-bottom cleaning.

Even in this short time, Henry had already lost several pounds. Just water weight, he liked to say coyly, but Lily thought it was more than that; his body was ready to release some of the burden.

"I like how the sunlight streams in, silhouetting the roses outside. It's so pretty and cheerful," Lily told Henry, admiring his efforts. "Looking through the window from inside makes me feel like Sleeping Beauty."

"Ah." Henry tucked the bandanna away and patted her hand. "And are there any princes planning on stealing you away? Huh?"

"No." Lily sighed, then laughed at herself. "Not yet."

He chuckled. "Those fools. But you're better off without them."

"I'll take your word for it." She smiled at him. When she'd arrived, she'd felt lonely and lost. Now, people cared about her—like Henry, Lily had found a family of the heart, full of uncles and aunts and even an adopted grandpa. She also very much liked Audrey and Zoe and Hazel, the younger women she'd met at the hotel at Beach and Forgotten. Lily didn't know them too well yet, but maybe, if she could spend more time in Mendocino, she could add some sisters of the heart to her new family.

"How's the old reading chair?" Henry clipped another leaf.

"Do you want to see? I just finished it. You can be the first one to admire my handiwork." She'd been working on upholstering the chair throughout the week, enjoying her new working space.

At first, the inside of the shed had been a mess—the floor had been claimed by rusted, dull garden tools, two defunct push mowers, several open packs of ancient fertilizer and gardening soil, and teetering towers of plastic pots that spoke of Grandma's planting efforts. From the ceiling dangled withered bunches of flowers dried so long ago they'd lost all color and fragrance, looking more like something out of a creepy movie than the cheerful sight they would have been when Grandma picked them.

With the help of her friends, Lily had cleared out the old stuff and freed the rafters from their dusty burden and the cobwebs, then hosed down the floors and walls. The sun dried the wash water, revealing the gorgeous redwood used to construct the shed. Alex built shelves for the walls and added a long workbench below the window. Beth arrived with an antique decorative mantel from her old house, which they put against the narrow end of the shed. While it wasn't a functional fireplace, it was a focal point and extra space for shells, books, and five Sterling silver bird figurines that were a shed-warming gift from Henry's store.

"I do want to see the chair," Henry said now. "It's been standing in my window for decades, reminding me of the good old days. I can't wait to see what you did with it."

She laughed. "Most of what I did you can't see. But it's very comfortable now, and I found a nice fabric for it at the flea market." She led him to the open door and helped him step into the cozy shed.

Golden light streamed into the rose-framed window, and the salty breeze seemed to flutter from window to door and back, delighted to play. In the middle stood the refinished chair. The warm wood glowed as if beaming with joy at its makeover. The new upholstery fabric was a soft, creamy yellow complementing the gorgeous wood, dotted with artfully embroidered honeybees, birds, and flowers. Lily loved the overall effect and couldn't wait to show her handiwork to Beth.

"I like it," Henry said appreciatively. "Your mom would've loved it. You're good at what you do. I'm proud of you, kid."

"Thanks. Mom loved anything with birds on it—china especially. But she'd have liked this fabric too." Lily gestured an invitation. "Try it out, Henry! Take a seat. It's got all new springs and stuffing."

"Ha, no." He huffed a laugh, making the little apron on his belly wobble. "I'm too big, Lily. It's still an old chair. The legs would give under all this carbonara and tiramisu." He patted his stomach.

"Ah, but they won't!" Smiling, Lily crossed her arms. "I'm a professional, after all. The chair is as solid as a rock. I'm going to be very offended if you don't at least try it out."

"Well then..." Henry shuffled over to the chair.

CHAPTER 30

Henry stood, still undecided. "Am I going to get your nice chair dirty?"

"No." Lily's smile deepened. She didn't just clobber new legs on old tabletops. She knew what she was doing and was proud of her skills. "I treated the fabric. You can spill a glass of red wine or squirt a ketchup bottle on it and wipe it off. It won't show."

"Huh." He touched the seat. "But it feels soft, not plasticky."

She opened her hands. "Of course it feels soft. Now, sit!" she commanded, growing impatient.

"Oh! Okay. On your word then." Slowly, Henry lowered himself into the chair. For a long second, he sat stiffly, not daring to move. Then, a surprised expression dawned on his round face, and he relaxed a little, looking up at her. "Not cracking!"

"Told you." Lily grinned, watching as Henry leaned back, then laid his hands on the soft armrests.

"It's so comfy," he said, wonder in his voice. "I don't think my body's been this comfortable since I was skinny. Something always hurts when you're old, you know? But not now. Not now at all." He started to stroke the fabric. "Look, a honeybee," he said and pointed at one of the little stitched creatures. "When Maggie was little, her dad—your grandpa—used to have bees in the garden." He tipped his head. "I forgot she told us about that. I forgot until just now."

Lily leaned against the workbench, looking out the window at the sea beyond the garden. "I didn't know that. I'd love to keep honeybees."

"Me too." Henry smiled, his beard twitching. "You know what?"

"What?" Lily turned back to him.

"Let's do it. Let's get some honeybees."

She smiled, a little sad. How she'd have loved to share that hobby with a quasi-grandpa... "That would be a great hobby for you! But I can't, Henry," she said softly. "I have to go back to Maine. Soon. In a couple of days. I have projects that can't wait any longer."

A look of disappointment flitted across his face, but he rallied quickly, smiling back. "Then I'll keep the bees. It'll be a reason to tackle my own backyard. And you come visit and help me extract the honey. We'll jar it for Beth and Mateo and everyone."

Lily swallowed, her eyes growing moist at the sweet offer. "I'd love that," she said. "I'll come back soon."

"Honey?" Beth had stepped into the shed without Lily noticing. "Oh, Lily, the chair looks great! And it fits Henry just so!"

Lily smiled. "Thank you, Beth. I'd like to give it to Henry while I'm gone if you don't mind. He says it's the only chair that makes him comfortable."

"That's a great idea." Beth nodded at Henry. "By the way, you did wonders with the roses out there. The shed looks like a little fairytale cottage."

"I like roses," Henry said a little sheepishly.

Beth slipped her arm through Lily's. "What were you saying about honey? Do you need some, Henry? I can fill you a pot to take home; I just bought a big glass at the farmers market. I bought way more than I meant to, but the beekeeper and I got to chatting so long about his work, I couldn't resist."

"Henry wants to keep bees in his backyard," Lily reported. "I think it's a great hobby to keep him active."

"Of course it'll take me a year or so to clear out my backyard." Henry laughed, slapping the armrests to show he was ready to make good on his intentions. "But it'll be good for me."

"Why don't you keep the bees here until you're set up on the island?" Beth suddenly suggested. "There's plenty of space behind the shed where they wouldn't bother anyone. We can point the hives so they fly out into the field instead of the direction of the house. It's nice and sunny...maybe too sunny... Oh, you could place the hives under the old oak! That would be enough shade. Also, the beekeeper at the farmers market said there can be heavy lifting; Mateo and I can help with that." She held out a hand, helping Henry stand without interrupting her planning. "And since you'll need to keep hives and boxes and frames somewhere, maybe Lily doesn't mind if you keep them in the shed here while she's in Maine?" Beth looked at Lily.

"I'd love that, actually," Lily said immediately. It was a great idea that would keep Henry moving and surrounded by company and friends. "It's such a nice space now, and it would be a pity to let it stay empty. Plus, it'll smell like honey and beeswax when I visit—always some of my favorite scents!"

"Really? I might have to check on the bees once or twice a week—I'll pay rent and let you have the honey." Henry looked from Beth to Lily, his face that of a little boy seeing his Christmas presents under the tree but still unsure whether he's allowed to finally touch them.

"Oh, fiddlesticks, rent. I'd love it," Beth said resolutely, hooking her arm under his. "Besides, you wouldn't be offering if you knew how much I paid for that jar of honey at the market! If I don't take care, you'll pretty soon start charging me!"

Delighted, Lily slipped her hand under Henry's other arm. "Beth really wants those bees, Henry. Say yes already."

"Yes," he said and huffed a laugh. "Yes, let's give it a go. I can leave the chair right where it is! I'll come over in the afternoons and sit in it at the open window, looking at my roses and listening to my bees."

"Fabulous." Beth looked very content as they walked out the door, supporting Henry across the single step. "Lily? Can you make dinner for yourself and Henry before he leaves? Mateo has everything ready in the kitchen for a seafood paella; you just need to throw it together and let it simmer for the flavors to infuse."

"Of course! I'll start it right now. Henry can help me." Lily beamed at Beth—the paella was one of her favorites, full of Mateo's flavorful mix of mussels, scallops, shrimp, succulent crab meat, flaky bites of fish, and tiny white calamari rings that perfectly balanced the creamy, savory, melt-in-the-mouth rice. "Is it time for the big family reunion?"

"Yes." Beth took a shaky breath, clearly nervous at the thought of the reunion. "Mateo is already at his house. I need to get ready and go over there now. He just texted that his sister and two brothers arrived early."

"Don't go," Henry advised wisely. "Have wine and paella with us in the garden."

"Oh, hush, Henry." Lily lightly slapped the old man's arm. "Of course she's going. Don't be nervous, Beth! They'll love you. His whole family will love you."

"Nobody's whole family has always loved anyone, kid," Henry said unhelpfully.

Beth swallowed, managing a weak smile. "It'll be all right," she said, sounding so pitiful that even Henry took mercy.

"I was just joking. Well—not really. But you can always just come back here, Beth."

"That's right—if anyone's mean to you, come back and we'll make a bonfire on the beach and watch the sun set in the ocean," Lily added. "But they'll love you. Don't worry."

"Right." Moistening her lips, Beth turned back, making her way to the house with only one or two short, doubtful pauses.

CHAPTER 31

B eth turned a last time before the mirror in the hall, scrutinizing her reflection. The dusty-rose color of the flowy dress Lily had talked her into buying complemented her light tan. Her hair, sparkling silver strands and all, fell to her shoulders, shining and healthy.

It was as good as it got.

Taking a last bracing breath, she stepped out of the house and into the happy warmth of a sunny afternoon. The walk to Mateo's house was only a short one, shorter along the street than the beach. By the time she reached his door, the shadows of the ancient oak trees shading his driveway were lengthening. She bit the inside of her lip, her heart fluttering in her chest.

Meeting the family was special. At least to her. She wanted his folks to like her, to decide that she was good for Mateo. In short, Beth wanted them to confirm that she was right for Mateo.

He'd already told her he didn't care what the family verdict was, but she knew better. Everyone cared about their family's opinion; that's just how human hearts were built. Everyone found it easier to have family on their side, leaning more joyfully into relationships that were gladly sanctioned by those who knew them best.

She rang the bell, hearing its chime reverberate through the house. She'd stayed over several times and loved Mateo's warm, easy, Mediterranean taste. It was luxurious yet deceptively simple, making everything convenient, comfortable, and pleasant while exuding the calm serenity of a lazy summer evening spent with friends.

Mateo opened the door. He was barefoot, the hems of his linen pants folded up and wet from the sea, his white shirt loose, the top button open. Clearly, they'd been on the beach, strolling in the water.

When he spotted Beth, his eyes widened appreciatively. "Bella! I was hoping it'd be you, but I thought you'd come down the beach." He stepped outside, offering her his hand.

Smiling, she took it. "Hi," she said, and with that one word, a lot of her doubt simply melted away. "It's good to see you, Mateo."

"You look like a painting of summer herself." He kissed her hand, then pulled her in for a real kiss. "Mmm. Kissing you makes me regret the house is full of family." He smiled, his gaze holding hers. "But they're out on the beach, drinking wine and eating bruschetta."

She nodded bravely, following him inside. "Who is here already? What are their names again?" Stepping on the cool terracotta tiles seemed to whitewash her brain.

"My sister, Sofia." He squeezed her hand reassuringly, leading the way. "And my brothers."

"Oh, of course. Sofia, Luca, Giovanni, Carlos. Sorry."

"Don't be sorry. Don't be shy, either. Just enjoy yourself." He stopped by the kitchen, pouring two glasses of wine and handing her one before they went out back.

"Mateo, it looks wonderful!" His garden was a little smaller than her own but professionally landscaped to be inviting and relaxing. Fragrant from the heat, laurel trees, rosemary, and lavender bushes scented the air. Gracefully arching olive trees, twinkle lights hidden in their branches, provided shade on the tiled terrace, where a long teak table was set beautifully with crystal and silver. White linens fluttered in the soft breeze, and vases with cheerful arrangements of pink and yellow roses, jasmine, lavender, and sprigs of green laurel dotted the space among platters and bowls offering appetizers.

Oleanders in full bloom and potted boxwoods framed the terrace. Just beyond its curved edge, citrus trees were heavy with lemons, oranges, and large, vibrant yellow grapefruits, which Beth knew made a perfect addition to breakfast.

In the distance, overlooking the beach, was a rectangular pool with a mosaic-tiled bottom and a roofed hot tub. A paved path led from the spa to the French doors of Mateo's bedroom, where a wide platform bed, draped in natural linen sheets, offered a view of the ocean.

Blushing at the thought of what they'd done there last night, Beth sipped her wine. Then she spotted the people on the beach. Mateo's siblings. They were talking and laughing among themselves, their backs to the house.

Mateo winked at her. "Everyone—Beth has joined us!"

"Ah! Aha!" A cheer rose from the four people who turned as one. Smiling, they raised their glasses in greeting, making their way out of the ankle-deep water.

"Hello." Beth couldn't help but smile and raise her glass back. His brothers looked like versions of Mateo, while Sofia, whom he liked to refer to as his baby sister, was a beautiful woman with silver threads in her raven hair that matched Beth's own.

"Beth!" Sofia walked straight up to her, lifted her glass out of the way, and gave Beth a long, one-warmed hug. "But you're gorgeous!" she exclaimed, stepping back to look Beth up and down. "Why did you make my poor brother wait so long? Years and years, he's been hoping for his angel to decide she wants him." Tipping her head, she smiled. "Now I know why! You look like a marble statue come to life!"

"Oh." Overwhelmed, Beth put a hand to her throat. "Really?"

"I told you!" Mateo was busy uncorking another bottle.

"Beth, welcome to the family." One of the brothers—Giovanni presumably, with his gray hair and silver temples—took her hand and kissed it. "I'm so glad I get to meet you."

"Thank you," she replied hastily, feeling like she should be more expansive and not knowing how. "Thanks. It's so nice to meet you!"

"You're lucky," another brother murmured out of the corner to Mateo before unceremoniously stepping up and kissing Beth on the cheek. "Sheesh," he said appreciatively, looking her up and down. "Well, my big brother always said he'd marry a looker when it was his time."

"Oh." Beth nervously ran her hands down her waist. "I don't know about—um. But thank you."

"Luca, quit it," Mateo called his brother to order. "Be respectful."

"I am! But...day-um, Matt. Now I know what all that fuss was about." Raising his glass, Luca winked.

Mateo shook his head at Beth, letting her know not to listen to that particular brother. Far from looking sorry, as he'd professed to be, Luca refilled his glass.

Smiling, the last brother held out a hand, and Beth shook. This brother looked most like Mateo and seemed closest in age. "You must be Carlos," she said, smiling back.

He nodded. "Glad to meet you, Beth. Mateo has mentioned you in our family chat before. He's been hoping you'd come to the restaurant so he could impress you."

"I see." Carlos's easy manner and Sofia's sisterly presence put Beth at ease. "What if I hadn't gone?"

Carlos raised an eyebrow. "As far as I remember, you were just about to accidentally bump into him at the farmers market." He cleared his throat. "And if you, theoretically, would have happened to buy apples, or oranges, or any fruit really, he'd have been there to help you pick them up."

Mateo sighed. "Had they spilled," he added. "It was just an idea."

"Of course." Carlos clapped a hand on his brother's shoulder. "Had they spilled. Otherwise, it would make no sense."

"Okay, I think that's probably enough." Mateo turned to the table, brushing his brother's hand aside. "Who wants—"

Just then, the chime of the front door echoed over the garden, making him pause. He straightened. "Ah! The cousins. Or...maybe my other guests."

"Maybe it's Antonia! I haven't seen her in ages! I'll get the door." Sofia, a gleam in her eye, unceremoniously pressed her glass into Luca's hand and strode inside without waiting for an answer.

Beth stepped closer to Mateo, curious. "I knew about the cousins, but...what other guests?"

Mateo smiled, wrapping an arm around her shoulders and pulling her close. "I had an idea this morning, and I'm not sure why I didn't think of it sooner—I invited your friends. Hannah, Sara, Alex, and since I couldn't get Sara without him, Andy."

"You did?" She looked up at him, her eyes widening. "But this is your family reunion, Mateo. Are you sure you want that?"

He nodded, setting down his glass and pulling her fully into his embrace. "I'm sure I want to make you happy, Beth," he murmured. "Your found family is my family."

He kissed the tip of her nose, his smile tender. "Besides, I like your friends."

She gazed up at him, marveling at her luck. "You really love me," she breathed, almost in disbelief that this man was hers.

"I love you," he murmured, closing the distance between them for a kiss that started a sweet, joyful tide of cheers and applause from family and friends.

Thank you for joining me in Mendocino Beach! If you're ready for more heartwarming moments and familiar faces, continue the story with **The Mendocino Reunion**!

MENDOCINO COVE SERIES

★★★★★ *"I loved it all, the history, the mystery, the sea, the love of family and friends...!"*

A gorgeous feel-good series with wonderful characters! Four friends are taking a second chance on love and life as they start over together in the small town of Mendocino Cove. Set on the breathtakingly beautiful coast of Northern California, where the golden hills are covered in wildflowers, vineyards grow sweet grapes, and the coast is rugged and wild. Start this charming sisterhood sage with The Hotel at Beach and Forgotten!

BEACH COVE SERIES

★★★★★ *"What an awesome series! Captivated in the first sentence! Beautiful writing!"*

Maisie returns to charming Beach Cove and meets a heartwarming cast of old friends and new neighbors. The beaches are sandy and inviting, the sea is bluer than it should be, and the small town is brimming with big secrets. Together, Maisie and her sisters of the heart take turns helping each other through trials, mysteries, and matters of the heart. Start this atmospheric series and read Beach Cove Home!

Bay Harbor Beach Series

★★★★★ *"Wonderfully written story! Rumors abound in this tale of loves and secrets."*

Lose yourself in this riveting feel-good saga of old secrets and new beginnings. Best friends support each other through life's ups and downs and matters of the heart as they boil salt water taffy, browse quaint stores for swimsuits, and sample pies at the Beach Bistro!

Start this absolute feel-good series with Seaside Friends!

About the Author

Nellie Brooks writes feel-good women's fiction about second chances, sisterhood, and hidden secrets. Her stories sweep you away to cozy seaside towns, where misty mornings and golden sunsets meet lively markets and salt-kissed shores. With lovable, down-to-earth characters, unexpected friendships, and tight-knit communities that rally around one another, her books feel like an invitation to escape—and come home at the same time.

Visit www.nelliebrooks.com for more feel-good series, sales, and updates!

Made in the USA
Middletown, DE
10 May 2025